Enjoy this book in good health

Edward Bruce Bew

Edward Bruce Bew

Death Takes a Honeymoon

DEATH TAKES A HONEYMOON

A potpourri of stories, essays and poems
by
Edward Bruce Bew

Cover by Mary Morrissey

Copyright ©2006 by Edward Bruce Bew

ISBN 1-4276-0245-X

All rights reserved. No part of this book may be used or reproduced by any means, graphic, electronic or mechanical, including photocopying, recording, taping, or by any information storage retrieval system without the written permission of the author, except for book reviews in recognized general-interest publications.

Author may be contacted by e-mail:
bewweb@earthlink.net.

Places, events and situations in this book are fictional. Any resemblance to persons living or dead is coincidental.

PRINTED IN THE UNITED STATES OF AMERICA
by
Ken Reed Printing, Inc..
475 Riomar Drive
Port St. Lucie, Florida 34952
Phone (772) 879-2727

DEATH TAKES A HONEYMOON
PRINCIPAL CHARACTERS

Roger Mangum and Nora O'Neal — High school lovers

George Evans — Classmate friend of Roger and Nora

Jean Wayland — Classmate antagonist of Nora

Caleb Mangum — Alcoholic father of Roger

Terrence and Maureen O'Neal — Parents of Nora

Erin O'Neal — Younger sister of Nora

Pearl Evans — Mother of George

Mimi Trent — Girl George marries

Matthew Wayland — Wealthy industrialist father of Jean

Victor Patarkis — Greek tycoon, Nora's first husband

Ted Patarkis — Victor's son, Nora's second husband

Lydia Patarkis — Ted's first wife

Demetrious and Eleni — Patarkis servants, Lydia's parents

Sherry Lord — Victor's mistress

Jose Garcia — Wayland Construction foreman, Caleb's friend

Nick Savage — Private Investigator hired by Jean

Leonardo — Old soldier Nora meets on Guam

Ibrahim — Corrupt Turkish official

Det. Sgt. Phil Webb — Policeman who finds Nora dead

TABLE OF CONTENTS

Death Takes a Honeymoon	5
The Agent/Manager	147
A Walk in the Past	151
The Fugitive	157
The Cad	161
My Life Will Never Be the Same	163
Love in Five Senses	170
The Fall	171
After the Fall (A sequel)	173
Coordinate, My Dear, Coordinate	177
Fortune Cookie Romance	181
It Started With A Kiss	184
The Girl On the Bus	185
Second Chance	189
Eulogy For a Friend	193
Back to the Beginning	195
Fire!	203
Dickens Would Twist In His Grave	205
Unanswered Prayers	208
One Small Step For Womankind	209
Hiding in Plain View	215
Agnu's Run	217
A Sailor's Lament	218

DEATH TAKES A HONEYMOON

CHAPTER ONE

There were not supposed to be any surprises on Roger's and Nora's honeymoon. After all, this was his second and her third, and they had "known" each other, in the Biblical sense, since high school days. More than five years.

But something odd did happen. Roger disappeared.

Nora was not aware of his absence. Her lifeless nude body lay in serene repose on the luxurious sateen sheets of the honeymoon bed.

* * * * *

The Year: 1999
The scene: Cocktail lounge of a plush oceanfront hotel in Miami Beach

Officer George Evans strolled over to the hotel bar and sat down beside Detective Sergeant Phillip Webb. "That was quite a send-off the captain got for his retirement, Phil. And did you see that classy SUV he got? When I retire I probably won't get so much as a used Yugo."

Phil laughed. "Oh, the guy's will chip in to buy you a pen and pencil set and a made-in-China 'Rolex' watch. And if I'm still around I'll try to find that Yugo for you." He took a sip of beer "Seriously, George, you're moving up in the department. You're a good cop and you just might retire as captain."

"Yeah, I like being a cop and so does Mimi."

"Where is Mimi? Didn't she come with you tonight?"

"No. She's expecting our first baby and she decided to stay home. I was Best Man at a friend's wedding yesterday and she was Matron of Honor. It was pretty tiring for her."

An obviously upset hotel desk clerk ran up to the two men. "Officers, we have a problem in seven twenty-four. A woman has passed out and there's no one there with her."

The policemen jumped up and followed the man as he hurried through the lobby, babbling as he ran. "Room Service got a call to send up a bottle of champagne. They were told to knock once and then go right in. When the waiter entered the room he saw a woman lying naked on the bed. He called out to see if there was anyone there and got no answer."

"Does anyone share that room with the woman?" Phil asked as they entered the elevator.

The clerk nodded. "Yes, her husband. They're on their honeymoon."

A sudden chill ran up George Evan's back. *Honeymoon couple? Oh, no.*

When the elevator stopped at the seventh floor the trio got off and hurried down the hall. The door to Room 724 was open wide, the doorway partially blocked by a service cart on which sat a silver bucket holding an ice-nested bottle.

"Looks like the Room Service man started to back out with his cart," Phil observed. With a quick shove he pushed the cart aside. He dashed over to the bed and placed a finger to the side of the throat of the woman lying there, held it a few seconds, then slowly turned away. "She's dead."

George stared at the still form and tears brimmed up in the corners of his eyes. "Oh, no, not Nora."

The sergeant looked up sharply. "You knew her, George?"

"Yeah. Her name's Nora O'Neal. No, I take that back. She just married Roger Mangum. The wedding I told you about." He stumbled to a chair, sat down and buried his face in his hands.. "She was Nora O'Neal when we all went to high school together. She was the queen of the senior class and
every guy in the school wanted her."

"Including you?"

DEATH TAKES A HONEYMOON

"Yeah, including me. But I never had a chance with her. Roger was the big man on campus and she went for him max time. She had grand ideas about what she wanted in life, and after high school she decided he didn't have enough ambition so she dumped him. She married another man. Actually, two other men. After Roger became a millionaire she finally married him." He paused and wiped his eyes. "I wonder where the hell he is."

"We'll put out an APB on him and get the crime scene boys up here. We don't know if he had anything to do with her death. Maybe somebody knocked him off, too"

Phil turned to the desk clerk still standing out in the hallway. "Don't say a word about this to anyone. We don't want a crowd of gawkers up here."

George went over and gently pulled a cover over Nora's lifeless body. "No need to have every cop in town ogling her."

DEATH TAKES A HONEYMOON

CHAPTER TWO

In the Spring of 1995 the 'trial of the century' murder trial of former football great O. J. Simpson was in full swing. A 6.5 magnitude earthquake in Greece caused massive damage but with little loss of life, but two weeks later an earthquake that hit the Russian town of Khabarovak killed 2000 people. An accident in a South African mine cost the lives of 104 miners. A New Zealand yacht beat the US defender for the America's Cup. A horse named Thunder Gulch won the 121st running of the Kentucky Derby. Jacques Chirac became President of France.

But the seniors at Central High paid little attention to world events. Their minds were filled with the basketball championship run, graduation just three months away, their futures — and Senior Prom.

George Evans rushed up to his friend. "Hey, Roger, I heard that Nora got kicked off the cheerleader squad. What happened?"

Roger Mangum shrugged his shoulders. "She told me she failed the physical. That's all she would say."

"I heard some of the girls say she's pregnant."

Nora O'Neal suddenly came around the corner. "You really piss me off, George, spreading such stupid rumors."

George's face crimsoned. "It's only what I heard."

"Well, you heard wrong," she snapped. She grabbed Roger's arm. "Come on, Roger, I want to talk to you."

They headed down the hallway and out the front door of the school. Once outside she confronted him. "Have you decided where you want to go to college?"

He didn't answer but continued walking.

She grabbed his arm and spun him around. Her eyes flashed.

DEATH TAKES A HONEYMOON

"Roger Mangum, when I ask a question I expect an answer. You have sent in applications, haven't you?"

He looked away. "I'm not going to college."

"You WHAT?"

"I'm not going to college. Jean Wayland's father is going to give me a job after graduation."

Nora's face darkened. "Have you been playing around with that uppity little tramp?" she demanded.

"Jean's not a tramp. She's really a nice girl, and I haven't been playing around with her. I just happened to mention in class that I liked working with my hands and she told me that her father is in the construction business and might give me a job. I went to see him and he promised to put me to work after graduation. You know, my dad's a carpenter."

"Need I say more?" Nora sneered. "Look, Roger, I'm going to college and make something of my life, and I have no intention of being tied to a loser. If you want to stay with me, you'd better straighten up and fly right."

CHAPTER THREE

Nora entered the outer office of Wayland Construction Co. and approached the receptionist. "I'm Nora O'Neal. I have an appointment with Mister Wayland."

"Oh, yes. I'll tell him you're here." She touched an intercom button. "Miss O'Neal is here, Mister Wayland."

"Send her in."

The receptionist looked up. "You may go in. It's the first door on the left down the hall."

Nora felt a tinge of apprehension as she approached the door to the private office. *Why in hell does he want to see me?* She tapped once and walked in.

Matthew Wayland greeted her with a broad smile. "Come in, Nora. Have a seat. Would you like coffee? Tea?"

Nora remained standing, her face impassive. "Nothing, thank you."

Wayland continued to smile. "I suppose you wonder why my daughter asked you to see me. Please sit down, Nora."

She sat gingerly on the edge of a chair facing him. "Yeah, I did wonder. Jean and I are not exactly the best of friends."

"I'll get right to the point, Nora. I am hiring a young classmate of yours, Roger Mangum, who I think can be trained to be of value to me. While he is in training I don't want him to be distracted in any way. I understand that you and he are involved in a little, er, high school romance..."

Nora broke in "Roger and I..."

Wayland stopped her. "Please let me finish, Nora." He gave her a depreciating smile. "As you probably know, these little high school romances usually end sooner or later. I think I can make it worth your while for this one to end sooner, not later."

DEATH TAKES A HONEYMOON

A crafty smile crossed Nora's face. "You want to pay me to dump Roger?"

"Dump is such a crude way of putting it. I just thought that when you go to college you would not want any distractions from your studies. You are going to college, aren't you?"

"Yes."

He leaned back and placed his hands behind his head. "I want to make you an offer, Nora."

"I'm listening."

"I want to pay all of your college tuition and give you a reasonable amount of spending money. Also, you'll have your own apartment off campus."

Nora smirked. "I'll have an apartment as long as Roger stays out of it, is that it? Level with me, Mister Wayland, is all of this because your uppity little daughter wants Roger?"

His face hardened. "Leave Jean out of this."

Nora shrugged. "I've had worse offers. Will you put the deal in writing?"

Wayland's smile returned. "I don't think that will be necessary, Nora. If I don't keep my end of the bargain you won't keep yours. I wouldn't want that to happen, would I?"

"All right, we have a deal." She paused. "I'll take that coffee now. No cream, two lumps of sugar, please."

He stood up and went over to a coffeemaker sitting on a bar in one corner of the office, filled two cups and handed one to Nora. "Oh, one more thing, Nora. You won't want to be hanging around town this summer so I've arranged a cushy job for you on a cruise ship."

Nora gave him an admiring smile. "You thought of everything, didn't you Mister Wayland? You were pretty sure I would take you up on your offer." She raised her cup. "Cheers."

CHAPTER FOUR

"Why don't you want to go the Senior Prom, dear?" Pearl Evans asked tenderly.

George looked down at the floor. "I don't have a date, Mom."

"Oh surely there are a lot of girls in your class who would give anything to go with my handsome son."

"There's only one that I want to go with and she's going with Roger Mangum."

Pearl put her arms around George and held him tightly. "I know how you feel about Nora, but if you miss this prom you'll regret it the rest of your life. Now put on your best suit and go over to that gymnasium and dance with every girl there." She paused. "Including Nora."

George hesitated. "Well, I guess I could. The boys aren't wearing tuxes this year but the girls are wearing formals."

His mother released him from her embrace and gave him a shooing motion. "Go. Go."

As George bounded up the stairs her gaze followed him wistfully *I wish he would forget about that Nora O'Neal.*

****

Roger picked up Nora at her home. "Wow, look at you!" he exclaimed as she came down the stairs, "you're a knockout in that gown. I never saw that one before. Is it new?"

"She thinks she's a knockout in anything she wears," Nora's younger sister grinned.

"Get lost, Erin," Nora demanded. She swirled around, the hem of the formal fanning out. "Like it, Roger? I just bought it today."

"Yeah, it's fantastic, but it looks like it cost a mint. I thought

DEATH TAKES A HONEYMOON

you were saving for college."

Her face darkened. "Roger Mangum, when I want something I get it."

****

The band was playing to a crowded dance floor when George entered the gymnasium. He spotted a group of boys off to one side and walked over to them. "You guys here without dates, too?"

One of them raised his chin in feigned arrogance. "We're playing the field, man. We get our pick of the chicks and we didn't even have to buy a corsage."

The music stopped and the Master of Ceremonies picked up his microphone. "Next dance is ladies' choice. All you gals grab a guy and LET'S DANCE."

Jean Wayland started toward Roger but Nora blocked her way. "He's mine until after graduation," she hissed in a low voice.

Jean didn't move for a long moment. She gave Nora a scathing glare then turned and walked to where the singles stood. "Will you have this dance with me, George?"

* * * *

The graduation ceremony was of the usual solemn pomposity. When it was over, Roger and Nora left together and drove to her home. She opened the front door. "Come on in, Roger. Mother and Dad went from the graduation to Erin's dance recital. There's no one home."

They ascended the stairs to Nora's bedroom. She carefully removed her cap and gown, folded the gown and placed the cap and gown on the seat of a chair. Slowly and methodically she removed all of her clothing and draped each piece over the back of the chair. Nude, she climbed into bed and lay spread-eagle on her back.

Roger feverishly stripped off his clothes, dropping them on the floor. He jumped into bed and lowered himself over her.

"Take it easy," she whispered, "give me a chance to warm up." She smiled inwardly. *Enjoy it, Roger, this will be the last time for you and me.*

* * * *

George Evans drove away from the graduation ceremony, his mother with him. On a sudden impulse he turned down the street where Nora lived and drove past her house. Roger's car sat on the driveway. *Just as I thought, Roger is there with her.*

"You must forget about that girl, George," Pearl Evans said softly, "she's no good for you."

CHAPTER FIVE

This is not exactly the giant luxury cruise ship I expected, Nora thought as she approached the *Caribbean Lady* lying alongside a dock at Port Everglades. *Hmm, no passengers getting aboard. Must not be close to sailing time.*

A smiling woman in her mid-thirties greeted her. "Hi, you must be Nora. I was told to expect you. Welcome aboard. I'm Sherry Lord, Concessions Manager. Just leave your luggage there. A porter will take it to your cabin."

Nora boarded the ship.

Sherry crooked a finger. "Come on, I'll show you around. This is primarily a gambling ship. We sail every Monday and return Friday. The ship is of foreign registry so we must touch at least one foreign port before returning to Florida. We spend one day and night in Nassau. The rest of the time we just sail around and let the passengers gamble. That's really what they take the cruise for."

"What will my job be?" Nora asked.

"You'll be working in the gift shop off the promenade deck. When we're at sea the shop is open from ten to four. It's closed when the ship is in port when most of the passengers go ashore. When you're off duty you have the run of the ship just as if you were a paying passenger. But stay away from the slots; they'll clean you." She led the way to a lower deck and opened a door. "This will be your cabin."

Nora looked around. The cabin was small but appeared to be comfortable. A bunk bed ran along one wall while the only other furniture, a small desk with a chair, sat beneath a single porthole.

"There's a vanity and shower behind that curtain," Sherry pointed out. She smiled. "I must warn you, there will be a lot of men knocking on your door. It's up to you as to whether you want to let them in."

A mischievous grin lighted Nora's face. "Do you open your door?"

Sherry laughed. "That's classified information." She took Nora's arm. "Come on, I'll show you how the gift shop works." She led the way back up to the promenade deck and into the shop. "All of the items have bar codes and the register reads them. Almost all of the purchases are with credit cards. I'll show you how to handle them. And I'll point out the items I want you to push. Any questions?"

"I think I can handle it. Where will I find you if I run into trouble?"

Sherry pointed to a door at the rear of the shop. "I have a small office back there. If I'm not there you might find me in the casino. As they say in the circus, I 'double in brass'. I'm a croupier at a roulette table."

Well, Mister Wayland, Nora thought, *the deal you gave me doesn't appear to be at all bad.*

DEATH TAKES A HONEYMOON

CHAPTER SIX

Jean Wayland intercepted Roger as he checked out at the end of a workday. "You are going to the company's Fourth of July picnic, aren't you, Roger?"

Roger looked at her in surprise. "I didn't know about a picnic."

"Oh, yes. Every year the company throws a picnic for the employees. The boys who aren't married team up with the girls who aren't married." She paused. "If you haven't met any of the single girls, you and I could go together."

Roger shifted his feet uneasily. "Well, sure. I don't have any plans for the Fourth." *Yeah, I don't have any plans for the Fourth. Nora left without even saying goodby.*

"Good. It'll be a fun day," Jean laughed.

A few days later Matthew Wayland drove up to a construction site and went over some blueprints with his foreman. Satisfied that the job was proceeding on schedule he looked around.

"How's that new boy I sent you doing, Jose?"

"Fine, boss. He good man. Work hard. Learn fast. Don't mind get hands dirty." He laughed. "Maybe he buckin' for my job."

Wayland gave him a slap on the back. "Don't worry, your job is safe. I've got other plans for him." He walked over to where Roger was working. "How's it going, son?"

"Great, Mister Wayland, I really appreciate your giving me this job."

"Well, Jose tells me you're coming along fine. Keep up the good work." He started to go then turned back. "Jean tells me you're going to the picnic with her. She's quite fond of you, you know. It

won't hurt to be nice to her." He headed back toward his car.
Roger stared after him. *Oh, God, what am I getting myself into?*

CHAPTER SEVEN

Nora found her first voyage on the *Caribbean Lady* to be exciting. Though business at the gift shop was brisk, she was never swamped. She found it easy to talk with the customers, especially the matronly ladies she convinced to buy outrageously loud, and expensive, island-motif blouses.

At four o'clock she placed the 'CLOSED' sign on the counter and went to her cabin to freshen up. Refreshed, she walked up to the promenade deck and strolled into the casino. She spotted Sherry behind a roulette table and wandered over to watch. A distinguished-looking gentleman was the only player.

"This is not my lucky day," he sighed, "I have need for a good luck charm." He glanced at Nora. "Perhaps this vision of loveliness will be my lucky lady and pick a winning number for me."

Nora blushed. "I don't know anything about roulette."

"Ah, then perhaps we could use your age. What would that be?"

"Nineteen."

The man placed a stack of chips on number nineteen. The wheel spun and the little marble bounced.

"Nineteen it is," Sherry called, and shoved a pile of chips toward him.

"Ah, that is more like it. Now, my lucky lady, what number should I play next?"

"How about playing YOUR age?"

"Ah, that I wish, but the numbers on the wheel go only to thirty-six."

Nora laughed. "Then play thirty-six. That would put it pretty close to your age."

DEATH TAKES A HONEYMOON

He beamed. "You are the little diplomat. No, I'll try to guess the age of our pretty croupier and play her age." He put his entire stack of chips on thirty-three. The marble danced around the whirring wheel.

"Double zero," Sherry called, "you were both wrong." Then with a smile, "You should never try to guess a woman's age, Mister Patarkis."

Victor Partarkis sighed. "All my chips are gone. I am such an unlucky gambler today but perhaps I could be luckier in romance." He smiled at Nora. "Would my lucky lady consider having dinner with me, and then we could dance away the evening afterward?"

Nora hesitated. "Well, I don't know." She felt a sudden urgency. "I have to go to the ladies' room. I'll think about it." She hurried away.

Sherry signaled to a relief worker to take over the roulette table and followed Nora to the restroom. She was waiting when Nora emerged from a stall. "That is one man you might consider opening your door to. He's Victor Patarkis. He's rich as Croesus and he's recently widowed. He's a major owner of this ship and he owns a charter airline." She paused. "He also has a fabulous home on one of the islands in Biscayne Bay."

Nora raised her eyebrows. "You seem to know a lot about him. You've been to his home?"

Sherry looked down at the floor. "Yeah, but it was just a one-night fling. There was really no chemistry there. But nothing could have come of it, anyway. I was married at the time and so was he." She gave a flippant toss of her shoulders. "I did get one thing out of it. I was working in the gift shop and I got promoted to the job I now have."

A sudden thought struck Nora. "Do you know a man named Wayland?"

DEATH TAKES A HONEYMOON

"Matthew Wayland? Sure, he's a part-owner of the Caribbean Lady."

Nora pursed her lips. *So, Mister Wayland, you're still trying to manipulate me. Well, two can play that game.* She looked at Sherry. "All right, I'll dance with your Greek tycoon."

The two returned to where a smiling Victor Patarkis waited. "I've decided that I will have dinner with you, Mister Patarkis," Nora said.

"Ah, you know my name, but I don't know yours."

"It's Nora. Nora O'Neal."

"Ah, Nora O'Neal. That's a pretty Irish name. But please call me 'Victor'." His eyes twinkled. "I suppose Sherry told you some preposterous lies about me when you two went to the ladies' room."

"She said you were rich as Croesus and that you dance divinely."

"Ah, Sherry is the little diplomat, too. But about dinner. Come to the first serving. The steward will show you to my table. Afterward we will see if your dancing equals your beauty."

As the time for the evening meal approached Nora took her new evening gown from its rack, the dress bought for the Senior Prom. She brushed it lightly and slipped it on. *I wowed Roger in this. I wonder if it will have the same effect on the distinguished Greek gentleman?*

A knock sounded on the door. "It's me, Sherry."

Nora opened the door. Sherry stood there holding an orchid corsage.

"Victor told me to pin this on you." She winked. "Play your cards right, kid, and you've got it made."

DEATH TAKES A HONEYMOON

When Nora entered the dining room Victor was already seated. He stood up as the steward guided her to the table. The steward pulled out a chair and Nora sat down. Victor returned to his seat.

"You are absolutely ravishing, my dear," he smiled, "some young man must be waiting breathlessly for your return from each voyage."

"I don't have a steady boyfriend. Besides, this is my first voyage."

"Ah, then I was the lucky one to be aboard the Caribbean Lady this trip. I sail on her only two or three times a year". He motioned for the steward to fill two wine glasses, then raised his glass. "A toast to my marvelous change of luck at the roulette table."

Nora raised her glass. "Cheers." She took a sip. "This tastes pretty good. What kind is it?"

"Dom Perignon. Yes, it is a good champagne. Now, what would you like to eat, Nora.? No. let me order." He flicked a glance at a waiter who hurried away.

"You already decided what we will eat, didn't you, Victor? Are you always so sure others will like what you decide?"

He smiled. "Why shouldn't they?"

The waiter returned with platters holding sizzling steaks. Nora began eating. "Umm. This steak is tender enough to cut with a fork. You have good taste in wine and in food, Victor.

He gave her an admiring smile. "And in women."

After an evening of dancing, Victor accompanied Nora to her cabin. She opened the door."Good night, Victor, I've had a fantastic evening."

"May I come in?" he asked softly.

She shook her head. "I hope you haven't gotten the wrong

idea about me. I'm not that kind of girl."

His face mirrored his disappointment. "But I will see you again?" He got a sudden inspiration. "We dock in Nassau tomorrow morning. I know of a Over the Hill club that has a terrific calypso band. Will you go there with me?"

"Over-the-hill club? Is that for old has-beens?"

"No, no, no!" he chortled. "You've never been to Nassau, have you, Nora? Most of business and government buildings are along Bay Street and around the harbor. There's a high ridge behind Bay Street. The working-class people live on the other side of the ridge. They call the neighborhood 'Over the Hill'."

Nora laughed. "All right, I'll go over the hill with you. What shall I wear?"

"Day wear in the islands is very casual. Just wear something that will show off your lovely hips and your..." He grinned. "Shorts and halter will be most appropriate. Take a wide-brimmed straw hat from the shop. I'll have Sherry put it on my bill."

Nora entered her cabin, closed the door and leaned back against it in exultation. *So, Mister Victor Patarkis, you want me. Well, I'll decide when or if I'll open my door to you.*

CHAPTER EIGHT

George Evans entered the living room, a dejected look on his face. "I passed the Civil Service Examination, Mom, but my application to the Miami Police Academy was rejected. They said the class is full but that I might be considered for a future class."

"Don't give up hope, dear," his mother consoled him. "You'll get in eventually. Meanwhile I'm sure you can find a job you will like."

"Well, I was talking to a fellow at the Academy. He drives for a limo service but wants to be a policeman. His application was accepted so he told me his old job would be open."

"You go right after it if that is what you want to do. You have the commercial drivers' license you got last winter at school when you became a junior volunteer with the ambulance service."

****

George shifted uneasily as the dispatcher at Patarkis Limousine Service examined his job application. The man looked up.

"You haven't had any experience driving a limo, have you?"

"No, sir, but I've driven an ambulance for the Volunteer Ambulance Service. It's almost as big as a limo. You see I got a Certificate of Proficiency." He pointed to a paper attached to the application.

"Well, Raul is leaving and I need a driver. Come on, let's see if you can handle a long car." He stuck out a hand. "I'm Carlos."

George got behind the wheel of the limo and Carlos sat beside him. "Hey, don't be nervous, man," Carlos laughed. "I'm not as hard to get along with as Mister Patarkis is."

"Mister Patarkis? Is he the boss?"

"Yeah. He's rich as shit and likes to throw his weight around. But he has a lot of irons in the fire and doesn't come to the office much. He lets me run things. Just kowtow to him when he comes in. He's not the most generous guy in the world but the pay is better than driving a hack."

CHAPTER NINE

Festivities were in full swing when Roger and Jean arrived at Crandon Park on Key Biscayne.

"Dad rented almost all of the picnic area for the day. Let's stake a claim to a table," Jean said.

As they raced from the parking lot Matthew Wayland called out. "Hey, Roger, do you play baseball?"

Roger stopped. "Yes, sir, I pitched for my high school team."

"Then come along. We're putting together teams from the construction workers and the office workers. I need a good pitcher for the office team."

"I'm not in the office, Mister Wayland. I'm in construction."

"You're in the office now. Next week you go to work in the Planning and Expediting Department."

"Come on, Dad, don't take him," Jean pouted. "We came to have fun together."

"You can have him later. Come with me, Roger."

The baseball game lasted throughout the afternoon, with lengthy 'time-outs' between innings so that the players could feast on the mountains of fried chicken, hamburgers and hot dogs coming off grills manned by caterers. Kegs of beer washed the food down.

As darkness fell, the picnickers prepared to watch the promised fireworks show. Jean spread a blanket on the grass and beckoned Roger to join her.

Promptly the sky lighted up with a scintillating display of pyrotechnics, accompanied by a crescendo of sound. Jean put her arms around Roger. "We could make beautiful fireworks together, Roger," she whispered.

Later, as they exited the parking lot, she snuggled up against

him. "You have a great future with the company, Roger."
    He stiffened.
    "Oh come on, relax. I don't bite." She took his right hand and guided it up under her tee shirt. "If you're still mooning over Nora O'Neal," she whispered, "forget her. She's gone. Let's go to my house. There's nobody home."

CHAPTER TEN

Victor left Nora's door, walked down a passageway and tapped on Sherry's door. "Are you decent, Sherry?"

"Wait a sec, I was about to step into the shower." She slipped into a filmy robe and opened the door. A faint smile crossed her face. "Struck out with Nora?"

He shrugged. "She will come around in time. What did you tell her about me?"

"The usual lies. You know, Victor, your lust for young women is going to get you in trouble. One of these days one of them is going to be too smart for you. So, what are your plans for Nora?"

His face brightened. "Ah, she might be a challenge. But in the end I will enjoy her luscious charms - - for as long as I find her amusing."

Sherry looked at him wistfully. "You and I know we can never marry as long as my husband is a vegetable in that nursing home. But I'm getting sick and tired of being your procurer."

"Be patient with me, my dear. You are my oasis in the desert, and tonight I am a thirsty man."

"Oh, all right," she sighed. She slipped off her robe and lay down on her bed.

Victor met Nora for breakfast the next morning. "Did you sleep well, my dear?"

"Yes, I got my beauty sleep. How about you?"

" I twisted and turned most of the night, and when I did go to sleep I dreamed about you."

"You really have a smooth line, Victor. You must practice it a lot," Nora laughed.

"And one so beautiful as you surely has had a lot of practice parrying smooth lines."

"There you go again! Right now I'm excited to see the sights in Nassau."

"Good. Would you like to take a walk after breakfast? We can visit the Straw Market and then take the staircase to the top of the hill. From there we can take a cab to the club."

"Straw market? Staircase?"

"The Straw Market is a place where the local people sell all kinds of things made by hand from straw. Hats, handbags, baskets, place mats and so forth. The Queen's Staircase is a stone stairway leading from downtown Nassau to Over the Hill. It was built to honor Queen Victoria and has sixty-four steps, one for each year of her reign."

Nora smiled. "You are a most charming tour guide, Victor."

A throng of shouting men greeted the passengers as they left the *Caribbean Lady*. "Taxi over bridge to Paradise," some called.

"Water taxi mo' fun, mon," others offered.

Victor waved them off.

"What's 'Paradise'," Nora asked.

"It's an island at the mouth of the harbor. We passed it coming in."

"Oh, that's where that big hotel we saw is?"

"Yes, a very large hotel with a very large casino. We don't encourage our passengers to go there. Not too long ago nothing was there but a beautiful beach, and the only way to get there was by boat. Now a bridge connects the island with downtown Nassau. You can go there by the bridge or you can still take the little water taxis."

After an exciting, for Nora, day on the island, she and Victor returned to the *Caribbean Lady*.

"You will have dinner with me tonight, and then dance a while, won't you?" Victor asked.

She gave him a faint smile. "Dinner and dance, that's all."

"You're playing hard-to-get."

"No I'm not. I just have my principles."

He shrugged in resignation. "All right, dinner and dance." He paused. "The ship is going for a routine inspection of her hull after this trip. It will be out of service for a week. Will you be a guest at my home for those few days? We can take Sherry along as chaperone. Actually, Sherry has been filling in as my party hostess since my wife and I, er, parted, and I have a party planned for the first night back. Nothing elaborate. Just thirty to forty friends and business associates. I've engaged a calypso band, not as good as the one Over the Hill, but adequate."

Nora thought quickly *Sherry told me she had been to his estate only once. She lied to me! Is she playing a game with me, too?* She gave Victor a light kiss on a cheek. "I'll think about it."

DEATH TAKES A HONEYMOON

CHAPTER ELEVEN

Nora, Sherry and Victor stood on the dock as passengers debarked from the *Caribbean Lady*. "Where's that dammed limo?" Victor fumed, "It was supposed to be here when we docked."
"Here it comes now," Sherry pointed.
The long grey sedan pulled to a stop and the driver got out.
"George!" Nora exclaimed.
George looked over quickly. "Nora?"
Victor's eyes narrowed. "You two know each other?"
"We were classmates in high school," Nora answered.
"Well, we don't have time for a class reunion. Put the baggage in the trunk, George, and you ladies get in the car." He walked to the rear of the car as George opened the luggage compartment. "You're new with the service, aren't you?"
"Yes, sir, I was hired this week."
"Do you know where you're to take us?"
"Yes, sir. Star Island, off the Venetian Causeway."
"Good. I'll show you my house when we get there." He turned and entered the car.
As the limo pulled out onto the highway, Sherry reclined in a captain's chair, her back to the driver, facing Nora and Victor, a bemused smile on her face.
"What are you smiling about?" Victor demanded.
"Oh, nothing." *So, now Nora's friends will know that she's hobnobbing with the big time crowd. This could be very interesting.*

When the limo pulled up to a magnificent waterfront estate, the passengers got out.

DEATH TAKES A HONEYMOON

"Unload the baggage onto the driveway, George," Victor ordered,"I'll have them taken inside. You're released." He turned to Sherry. "Find Nora a room. I'm going to the office for a while but I'll be back before the party starts. Everything has been taken care of for the party." He walked toward the garage.

"This place is fabulous," Nora awed as she and Sherry entered the house. "It looks like pictures I've seen of Hugh Hefner's mansion."

"Well, don't start getting ideas about living here. Victor has a short attention span for his playmates."

"I'm not his playmate," Nora retorted, "but you seem to have stuck around for a while."

"Victor and I have a business relationship."

"Is that all?"

Sherry didn't answer as she led the way up a winding staircase. She opened a door. "This will be your room while you're here. My room is just down the hall."

So, Nora thought, she has a permanent room in this fantastic playhouse. She looked around the spacious room assigned to her. A magna-size round bed sat between two windows overlooking the bay. Nora glanced upward. *Mirrored ceiling. That figures.* She crossed the room to the bathroom. A large sunken marble tub occupied one end while a double vanity took up much of the opposite wall. Between them sat a toilet bowl which Nora quickly noted had a bidet.
.   *Yes, Victor Patarkis, I think I'm going to like living in your playboy mansion.*

When Nora glided down the stairway, radiant in her evening gown, she saw that many guests had already arrived. The band was playing a tango. As she spotted Victor and started toward him she felt a light touch on her arm.

DEATH TAKES A HONEYMOON

"Will you have a dance with me, Nora?"

She spun around. "I didn't know you would be here Mister Wayland!"

He smiled. "Victor Patarkis and I are old friends". He took her arm and led her to the dance floor. They began to sway to the beat of the music. "So, Nora, " he asked. "Do you like your job?"

"Oh yes. I've made only one trip but I found the islands fascinating and I've met some exciting people."

He glanced toward Victor. "Yes, I see that you have." When the music stopped he guided her to the bar. "What would you like, Nora?"

"Dom Perignon"

"You've already developed a taste for the expensive bubbly, haven't you?" he smiled. He motioned to the bartender to fill two glasses. "You know, Nora, right from the start I figured you to be a smart girl but I never dreamed you could move this fast. You might have a little trouble reeling in the Greek tycoon."

She gave him an impish grin and raised her glass. "Cheers."

He continued to smile. "You know, Nora, I think I'll hang around to see how this little drama plays out."

"So, you're enjoying this game we're playing as much I am?"

He opened his eyes wide in feigned surprise. "Just what game are you referring to, my dear Nora?"

"You know what I mean. When you got me the job on the Caribbean Lady you knew that Victor would be aboard and that he has a liking for young women. He probably would not have taken that trip if you had not told him about me."

Matthew Wayland's eyes twinkled. He raised his glass. "Cheers."

Late in the evening, after the last of the guests departed, Nora gave Victor a light goodnight kiss and went to her room. As she undressed and prepared for bed a knock sounded on her door. "It's me, Victor."

She opened the door and stepped aside.

From up the hall, her door open a tiny crack, Sherry watched. *Well, Victor, it looks like you've made it with Nora. I wonder how long this one will last.*

The next night Nora moved into Victor's room.

The week passed in a dizzying kaleidoscope of motion. Sailing on Victor's yacht, clambakes on the beach, a trip to a shopping mall where Victor handed Nora a credit card and told her to 'go wild'. And there were nights when Victor displayed an amazing virility for a man his age.

On Monday morning Victor, Nora and Sherry had breakfast together. "You ladies will go back to the Caribbean Lady for the usual five-day cruise," he told them."I'll have you brought back here when the ship docks Friday." He glanced at his watch. "The limo will be arriving shortly. You should be getting ready to leave."

When a voice on the intercom informed Nora that the limo had arrived she hurried from her room. Sherry met her in the hallway. "I'm not going with you, Nora. I have something to take care of in town. I'll drive up to Port Everglades later this morning."

George was waiting beside the limo when Nora emerged from the house. He opened the trunk and put her bags in. "Not as much luggage as you had coming down," he observed.

"I left some things here."

"Oh." He looked toward the house. "Is anyone else going?"

"No, only me."

"Would you like to ride up front with me? We could talk."

DEATH TAKES A HONEYMOON

She glanced around apprehensively, then jumped into the front passenger seat and quickly closed the door. George got in, started the motor, and slowly pulled out of the circular drive.

They drove for several minutes before George broke the silence. "I saw Roger a couple days ago. He asked if I'd seen you around."

"He knows I have a job on a cruise ship."

"Well, he asked anyway. I didn't tell him I brought you to Star Island."

"Roger and I are history. I'm marrying a man who really amounts to something."

"Has Mister Patarkis proposed to you?"

Nora pursed her lips. "No, but he will."

CHAPTER TWELVE

Sherry Lord drove into the parking lot of the Sheltering Arms nursing home and came to a stop. For a long time she sat there, dreading to go inside. Finally she got out of the car, squared her shoulders and entered the building. A nurse greeted her. "Hello, Sherry. How have you been?"

"Just so so, Marie. How is he doing?"

The nurse's face sobered. "There's been no change. Once in a while an eye might move but that could be a reflex action. Come on if you wish to see him. Doctor DeVoe wants to speak with you before you leave."

They entered a Spartan room where a gaunt figure lay under a pristine white sheet. An oxygen tube entered his nostrils and a feeding tube disappeared beneath the cover. Sherry walked over and carefully wrapped her arms around the man. "Wake up, Dick, it's me, Sherry," she whispered. "Please wake up."

Dr. DeVoe came in and gently pulled her away. "He doesn't hear you." He guided her from the room and to a sofa in the reception area, and sat down beside her. "You must face the reality that your husband is brain-dead, Missus Lord. The brain cannot survive without oxygen as long as his did in that diving accident." He paused and then continued almost in a pleading voice. "I know we've been through this a dozen times but I feel I must once more try to make you see the hopelessness of his condition."

"Can't there be even the slightest hope, Doctor DeVoe?"

The doctor sighed. "There have been cases where a person has come out of a coma after five, ten or even fifteen years, but it's extremely rare. In your husband's case my professional opinion is that there is absolutely no chance. If you will allow us to remove the feeding tube his body will, in a very short time, peacefully join his brain in death."

    Sherry shook her head. "I can't do it. I can't do it." She looked up sharply. "You are receiving the payments for his care, aren't you?"

    "Oh yes. Mister Patarkis gave authorization for direct withdrawals from one of his bank accounts."

    Sherry smiled weakly. "I suppose Victor feels some responsibility for Dick's accident. Dick was diving from Victor's yacht and using Victor's equipment. Victor could have been the victim if he had gone out that day." She paused. "I'll never understand why Dick went down so deep with a near-empty air tank. Police who investigated the accident said the tank had a defective air gauge." She got up to leave. "I'll try to make up my mind to let you do what you think best. It will be a hard decision. Very hard."

DEATH TAKES A HONEYMOON

CHAPTER THIRTEEN

In the ensuing weeks a routine developed. After each cruise Nora and Sherry returned to the Star Island estate. The limousine service no longer picked them up; Sherry kept her car in a long-term parking lot near the dock. One day as they drove south on Interstate 95 Nora was unusually quiet.

"What's the matter, kid," Sherry asked, "getting tired of the playmate role?"

Nora's voice quavered. "I'm pregnant, Sherry."

"Oh, God, are you sure?"

"Pretty sure."

"And I don't suppose you've told Victor?"

"No. I'm scared. How do you think he'll take it?"

Sherry paused for a moment. "I've known Victor a long time. He has a gigantic ego and might be proud to father a child at his age. He might take full responsibility for the baby and put you up in an apartment where he'll have visiting rights. Before and after the baby is born." *Ha! Like hell. He'll insist on an abortion, pay you off and send you packing.*

"That's not what I want. I want to marry him."

"Don't be ridiculous!" Sherry scoffed. "He'll never marry you."

Victor's reaction to the news fell far short of anything Nora had hoped. "How could you be so dammed stupid!" he shouted. "You'll have to get rid of it. I'll have no bastard child."

"I can't have an abortion. My religion won't allow it."

"Your religion?" he sneered. "I've never seen you show the least bit of interest in religion."

"I'm devout in my own way. But look at the positive side. You would be proud to be the father of a beautiful baby, wouldn't you? You do find me exciting, don't you? I would be a good wife to you, Victor."

He looked at her sharply, then stomped out of the room without answering.

That night Victor came to the bedroom he and Nora shared. She was already in bed. She looked at him plaintively. "Don't be angry with me, Victor. You know I love you." She held out her arms. "Come give me a big kiss."

He began to undress. "I've decided to make you my wife, Nora. But my attorneys will insist that there be a prenuptial agreement. I'm involved in many businesses with different partners and my associates would not like the possibility of a novice taking over my interests at the time of my death."

"I don't want your money. I just want you," she whispered.

She found it hard to conceal her elation as he slipped into bed with her. *I'll see that the pre-nup is generous to me.*

In her room a few doors down the hall, Sherry, unaware of Victor's decision, tossed restlessly. *He can't marry that scheming little bitch. She would make life a living hell for him.* The next morning she called the nursing home. "Doctor DeVoe? This is Sherry Lord. I've decided to wait one more month to see if my husband's condition improves. After that you may do whatever you think is best
"

DEATH TAKES A HONEYMOON

CHAPTER FOURTEEN

Nora and her sister, Erin, went together to select a wedding gown. "I'm really happy that you picked me to be your Maid of Honor, sis," Erin smiled.

"Well, you always were a snotty little brat but you are family." Nora gave Erin a quick hug. "I'm proud to have my kid sister as my Maid of Honor."

They looked through the gowns on display. "This one is pretty," Erin suggested.

Nora glanced at the price tag. "Nope, too cheap." She waved a credit card. "I want only the best. Victor is paying for everything."

Erin shook her head. "You really are something else, Nora. You really are something else." She paused. "Just be sure you don't get something too tight, if you know what I mean."

Nora tossed her shoulders. "We're having a short engagement. I won't be showing much by my wedding day. But it really won't make much difference; when the baby arrives everybody in the universe will start counting on their fingers."

"Now that Dad has refused to have anything to do with your marriage to Victor, who are you going to have give you away?" Erin asked.

Nora's brow furrowed. "I know Dad wanted me to marry in our church, but he doesn't have to be so damned stubborn." Then her eyes danced mischievously. "I think I'll ask Roger Mangum to give me away"

"You wouldn't! Seriously, who are you going to get?"

"I already asked Uncle Amos. He agreed to do it."

They browsed for several minutes before Erin spoke again. "Do you ever wish that it's Roger you're marrying?"

DEATH TAKES A HONEYMOON

"Roger is a loser."

"I always liked him. I think he's a pretty cool guy."

"Well, if that uppity Jean Wayland hasn't already snared him he's open game. Go for it."

Erin gave her sister a steely stare. "I just might do that."

****

At the rehearsal dinner Matthew Wayland collared Nora during a lull in the activities. He gave her an admiring smile."I never thought you'd pull it off, Nora. I got to hand it to you." He paused "You know Victor picked me to be his best man. I don't know whether he's thanking me or blaming me for bringing you two together."

Nora gave a flippant toss of her head. "Oh, he'll thank you, and thank you, and thank you. So how is your uppity little daughter doing with Roger?"

Wayland's face darkened. "Never use that word when referring to Jean, Nora. She and Roger are dating and I think she will eventually make him forget you." He stopped and a frown creased his forehead. "I just wonder if you will ever really forget him."

CHAPTER FIFTEEN

Caleb Mangum swayed a little as he approached his son at a construction site. "Hey, Roger, I need a little help, boy. I got laid off and need a job. I thought you could get me one with Wayland."

Roger looked at his father in disgust. "Drinking on the job again?"

"Aw, I just had a couple beers at lunch. But I was gonna quit that job, anyway. They're a bunch of bastards to work for."

"Yeah, they're always 'a bunch of bastards'." Roger heaved a heavy sigh. "Jose does the hiring on this job. I'll see if he can use you. Come back in the morning – sober. And get one thing straight. You make me look bad and you're history, even if you are my father. I'm in Planning and Expediting now and came to this site to go over some blueprints with Jose. I've got a big future with this company and I'm sure as hell not going to let you louse it up."

CHAPTER SIXTEEN

Erin led the bridal procession, eyes straight ahead, her face an impassive mask. Nora, on the arm of her uncle, followed, a broad smile on her face. Sherry stood at the left side of the altar while Victor, with Matthew Wayland beside him, waited on the right.

Most wedding ceremonies adhere to a rigid time-honored formula, and this one followed tradition with one almost-undetected blip. When the minister intoned "If anyone has reason that this couple should not be joined in holy matrimony let him speak now or forever hold his peace." Sherry took a half-step forward and opened her mouth as if to speak. Then, her face flushed with embarrassment, she stepped back. *Yes, I could give a thousand reasons why he shouldn't marry this girl.*
With all eyes on the bride and groom, no one appeared to notice the fleeting episode.

Vows were exchanged. The minister pronounced them husband and wife, and Victor kissed his bride.

In the reception line in the foyer of the chapel, immediately following the ceremony, Wayland shook Victor's hand and asked "May I kiss the bride?" He embraced Nora tightly and planted a firm kiss on her lips. "Congratulations," he whispered into her ear.

Nora's eyes sparkled as she whispered back, "Cheers!"

The tabloids had a field day with accounts of the wedding of 'the Greek tycoon and his child bride'. But the main-stream media gave the event the royal treatment. Elaborate coverage, with many photographs, graced the pages of the society sections of local newspapers the day after the wedding. Even the space-starved evening news programs on television managed to budget thirty seconds for the event, playing up the couple's fairy-tale meeting and their planned romantic honeymoon in the Greek islands.

DEATH TAKES A HONEYMOON

The following day a brief announcement appeared on the obituary page of the *Miami Herald*.

Richard Lord, 37, of Miami died September 9 after a long illness. He is survived by his wife, Sherry. Funeral plans have not been announced.

The tabloids didn't miss the event. They struck swiftly with their usual vicious innuendo.

HUSBAND OF FINANCIER'S MISTRESS DIES 10 YEARS AFTER SUSPICIOUS DIVING ACCIDENT PUT HIM IN COMA

Nora and Victor did not see the lurid headlines; they were high in the skies above the Atlantic Ocean on their way to Greece.
.

Victor had not asked Nora where she wanted to go on their honeymoon. In a matter-of-fact tone he announced "We'll go to my old home on Samos. It's a beautiful island. You'll love it." Then he added. "I can take care of some business matters while I'm there."

As the commuter plane cruised low over the island-dotted sea on the hour-long flight from Athens to Samos, Nora began to feel the excitement of this ancient, but to her, new, world. "The view is absolutely spectacular," she whispered to Victor. "I wouldn't have missed it for the world."

Victor beamed at her exuberance. "Wait until you see Samos. In Greek mythology, Hera, wife of Zeus, was born there. She was the Goddess of Fertility and Nature, and she endowed her home island with a salubrious climate and lush vegetation. Some of the finest Greek wines are produced there."

Nora wrinkled her nose. "I don't know anything about Greek mythology but that wine part sounds interesting. Is Greek wine as tasty as Dom Perignon?"

"Dom Perignon is a French champagne. But you'll like the wines of Samos. In time, my dear, you will learn to understand and appreciate good wines – and Greek mythology." He thought for a moment. "I must see to it that the steward aboard the Caribbean Lady puts in a variety of Greek wines."

"There you go thinking business again," Nora smiled. She paused. "What will I use for money when I go shopping?"

It was Victor's turn to smile. "There you go thinking shopping again. Greek currency is the drachma. Sadly, because of inflation it is worth very little. American dollars and credit cards are accepted everywhere."

At Aristarhos International Airport a car awaited them. A porter loaded their luggage into the trunk then opened the passenger-side door for Nora. Victor slid in behind the steering wheel. "My place is only a short drive from town," he told Nora.

They drove through a picturesque village, its streets lined with small shops and sidewalk vendors. Tourists, their ubiquitous cameras identifying them as though they wore tee shirts emblazoned 'Tourist', were everywhere. As Victor drove past a long line of seafront hotels, he waved a hand around. "Samos has some small manufacturing plants, and fishing and agriculture are important industries, but tourism brings in the most money. As you learn to know the island you will see why its charms attract so many people, dear."

Dear, Nora thought. *He rarely calls me any affectionate names. Could it be that back in his own environment Victor is becoming less stiff and formal?*

They left the village and took a serpentine road that wound along the coast. Below, on the right, fishing boats rested on sun-drenched beaches, the fishermen busily repairing nets. Offshore, luxury yachts lay at anchor or scudded along in the brisk breeze. On the left the tree-covered mountain rose sharply, its sides adorned with large and small homes, like ornaments on a Christmas tree.

After driving a few kilometers Victor pulled off the road and onto an overlook. He stopped the car. "Come on, Nora, let's get out.

DEATH TAKES A HONEYMOON

I want to show you something." When they emerged from the car he put his arm around her waist and pointed upward. "See that villa way up there? That's where we're going."

Nora gasped. "How in the world will we get there?"

He laughed. "We won't have to climb the mountain. The road winds around and passes just below it. There is a courtyard with servant's quarters just off the roadway, and stone steps lead up to the main house."

"Like the Queen's Staircase in Nassau?" Nora's eyes sparkled.

"Somewhat," he smiled, "but not nearly as many steps."

They got back into the car and continued on. At a sharp curve in the road Victor suddenly tensed.

"What is it?" Nora asked in alarm.

"Nothing. Nothing." But his jaw set in a hard line.

When they drove into the courtyard of the villa Nora could see two people waiting. "They're Eleni and Demetrius, my household staff," Victor told her. "They've been with me for many years. They speak fairly good English so you won't have a problem communicating with them. My first wife was American. She spoke almost no Greek at first so they learned English."

"You keep the place open even when you're away for months, even years?"

"My son, Theodore, and his wife live here. But don't worry; we'll have the place to ourselves while we're here. He's off climbing mountains in Tibet or some place and his wife is at a retreat."

"Retreat? Is she a religious person?"

Victor hesitated. "Lydia is addicted to drugs and alcohol. From time to time she goes to a rehab clinic for a cure."

Demetrius greeted them with a beaming smile. He spoke a few words in Greek then switched to English. "So good you back to

DEATH TAKES A HONEYMOON

Samos, Meester Patarkis, an' you bring beautiful bride."

Eleni gave Nora a warm hug. "You weel luv Samos as we do."

Victor gave the servants instructions in Greek and took Nora's arm. "They will bring our bags. Let's go on up. Watch those steps. They can get slippery."

They ascended the long stone staircase and emerged on a patio overlooking the far-below sea. "This place is breathtaking," Nora marveled. "Have you lived here long?"

"My father brought me here when I was just a boy. But let us go inside."

They entered a low-ceiling foyer that led to a spacious living room with a high, domed ceiling, a room furnished in classic Greek style, with reclining lounges facing a massive fireplace that dominated one end of the room. A curved flight of steps led to a balcony surrounding the living room. "The bedrooms all open from the balcony," Victor indicated with a wave of his hand.

Nora's eyes opened in amazement. "This place is fantastic, Victor. I feel like I'm living in a fairy tale."

He smiled. "Well, you are my fairy-tale princess."

Demetrius brought in some of Nora's luggage. Victor spoke a few words in Greek, then turned to Nora. "Follow him. You can start unpacking. I will be up later."

Nora started to follow the servant then abruptly changed her mind and turned back. She spotted Victor standing on the terrace, both hands clenched on the wrought iron railing, silently staring at the scene below.

Nora walked over and put an arm around him. "A drachma for your thoughts, Victor."

He gave her a wan smile. "Ah, you are becoming Greek already." He put one hand on her waist and with the other hand pointed downward. "See that road below? That's the one we came up on. My wife was killed on that road."

"Oh, how terrible," Nora gasped.

"She was driving too fast and lost control on a curve. I was sitting beside her but was thrown free. She went over the embankment. That was ten years ago."

Nora's eyes widened. "Sherry said you were recently widowed."

He laughed. "Sherry does not always tell the complete truth."

"Yes, I've already discovered that. I have a feeling that there's more to your relationship with her than either of you have told me." She frowned. "I know so little about your past, Victor."

"And I know so little about yours. But at your age there is not so much past to know about, is there?"

He abruptly changed the subject. "Would you like to go to Turkey, Nora? I have a business matter to take care of in Kusadasi. It's a ninety-minute trip by ferry from Samos, a very pleasant ride. I have taken it many times and never tire of it."

"Are there any good places to shop?"

Victor smiled. "Yes, it is a tourist destination. There are many small bazaars selling mostly native crafts, costume jewelry, artifacts and Oriental rugs. But do you ever think of anything but shopping?"

She jabbed him playfully in the ribs. "Do you ever think of anything but business?"

He gave her a quick hug. "Tomorrow we go to Kusadasi. But we are on our honeymoon. Tonight we make love."

The next morning, with Demetrius sitting in the rear seat, they drove into Samos Town. Nora's eyes opened wide when she saw the ferry. "It's almost as large as the Caribbean Lady," she exclaimed, "I expected something like the Staten Island ferries I saw when I went to New York. Do you own this one, too, Victor?"

"No, no, no," he laughed, "The Caribbean Lady is my only

ship, and I don't own all of her. But the Lady is small for a cruise ship. She is mostly a gambling casino."

When the ferry docked at the Turkish port they disembarked and Victor led the way to a waterfront restaurant with an expansive table-filled veranda. "We will meet here for lunch, Nora, and then take the afternoon ferry back to Samos. My business matter will be taken care of by then. Demetrius will guide you around."

"What will I use for money?" Nora asked.

"The shops will honor your credit card. You don't want to buy from the sidewalk vendors. They will rob you blind."

With Demetrius following a step behind, Nora roamed through the bazaars, excitedly examining articles that caught her fancy. At one shop she picked up a silver necklace. "This is pretty," she said to Demetrius.

"No, Missy," he warned, "From Kibris. Mister Patarkis no want you buy."

"Well, I like it," she answered defiantly. She handed her credit card to the smiling merchant.

He glanced at the card and suddenly flew into a rage. "Patarkis!" He pulled a scimitar from under his counter and began waving it wildly and screaming at them in Turkish.

Demetrius grabbed the credit card from the man and tugged at Nora's elbow. "Come, we go."

"What was that all about?" Nora demanded.

"Mister Patarkis tell you."

They hurried to the restaurant where Victor awaited them. Demetris rushed up to him babbling in Greek. Victor's brow furrowed.

"Will someone please tell me what's going on?" Nora pleaded.

"The shopkeeper is a Turkish Cypriot. We had better get back to the ferry before he starts a riot."

DEATH TAKES A HONEYMOON

"He called your name before he blew his stack, Victor. Why is he angry at you?"

"It's a long story. My father led a band of Greek insurgents in the fighting for Cyprus's independence. The Patarkis name is highly respected in the Greek part of the island, but not in the Turkish-occupied north end."

"There was much killing?"

Victor shrugged. "It was war."

"And there was looting?"

For a moment Victor hesitated. "Yes, there was much looting of the Turkish sector."

"Was that the beginning of the Patarkis fortune? Loot from Cyprus?"

His features hardened. "I made my money honestly in the transportation business. My father never mentioned where he got his money."

As they boarded the ferry, Victor chuckled. "So, Nora, how did you like Turkey?"

She brushed past him. "I didn't buy one little thing. Let's get away from here while we still have our heads."

The ferry pulled away from the dock and began its trip to Samos. The passengers included several fez-wearing Turkish businessmen, apparently going to the island to buy wine, fruits and vegetables. Nora shrunk back when any of them strolled past. Victor cradled her in his arms, as a parent would a frightened child. "Do not be afraid, my dear, they will not harm you. Most Turks are quite friendly. You just happened to run into one from Cyprus who holds a grudge against my family."

Nevertheless, Nora did not relax until they reached the safety of the villa.

The next morning as they were having breakfast on the terrace,

DEATH TAKES A HONEYMOON

Nora sniffed the air. "Do you smell smoke, Victor?"

He looked up sharply and sniffed. "Yes, I believe I do."

Demetrius rushed up the staircase and spoke to Victor in Greek. "The forest is on fire in the hills above us. I heard on the radio. Police say people should leave here."

Victor pushed back from the table. "Hurry and pack a bag with what you'll need for a few days, Nora. Sometimes these fires get out of control. We'll go to a hotel until it's safe to return."

They rushed to the bedroom, packed, and returned to the terrace. Demetrius took the bags down to the car.

"What about Demetrius and Eleni?" Nora asked.

"They have a car. They will leave."

Nora ran toward the staircase.

"Careful," Victor repeated his earlier warning, "Those steps can be slippery."

As she started down she suddenly clutched at her breast, "Help me, Victor, I feel faint."

He dashed toward her but before he could reach her she slumped over and rolled down the stone steps.

Victor bounded to where she landed and took her in his arms. "Nora, Nora, are you hurt?"

She did not answer.

With Demetrius' help he placed her limp form in his car. He got behind the wheel and roared off toward the hospital in Samos Town.

Victor paced the floor anxiously as the emergency room staff worked to revive Nora. Finally a doctor approached and spoke to him in Greek. "Your wife does not appear to be seriously hurt. There are no broken bones or concussions, just numerous abrasions. She appears to have fainted. Probably from the excitement of the fire and..." He paused and placed a hand on Victor's shoulder. "I am sorry that I must tell you that she lost the baby she was carrying."

Victor took a sharp breath. "May I see her now?"

"She is being admitted for further observation. You may see her for a moment here, and then visit her in her room later."

When Nora felt strong enough to travel, Victor insisted that they return to the Star Island estate. "The flames did some damage to the villa, and the woodlands on all sides are scorched. It will not be a pleasant place to live for awhile. I contacted Theodore. He is cutting short his climbing expedition and coming home to look after the repairs."

DEATH TAKES A HONEYMOON

CHAPTER SEVENTEEN

During the two years following the wedding of Nora and Victor, Roger Mangum rose rapidly in the Wayland Corporation, and his father, Caleb, managed to remain sober enough to hold his job with the company and to rise to a foreman position. Erin O'Neal graduated from high school and completed one year at community college. George Evans received an appointment to the Police Academy. Sherry Lord continued to work as Concessions Manager on the *Caribbean Lady*, and Victor made frequent inspection trips aboard the ship, always finding excuses as to why Nora could not accompany him.

Nora and Victor had been married for two years but the honeymoon had long since ended.

****

George Evans stirred uneasily at his desk as his first class at the police academy was about to start, his face a mask of apprehension. A young woman sitting next to him smiled.

"Hey, relax. The worst they can do is kill you."

"No talking in class," the instructor barked. He glared at them. "The only one to talk in this class is me, unless you are asked a question. Is that clear to all of you?"

A murmur of assent arose from the class.

"I am Sergeant Duncan," the instructor continued, "You are here to learn to be policemen. This is not a boy-meet-girl meeting place. And you will learn to be good policemen. I promise you." He emphasized "promise".

George's nervousness subsided as the morning sped by but he was glad when lunchtime came. In the cafeteria he filled a tray and headed for a table. His classmate was already seated. She called to him.

"Want to join me?"

A grin lighted George's face. "Do you think Sergeant Duncan will allow it?"

"Screw Sergeant Duncan."

George sat down across the table from her. "Our teacher acts like a Marine Corps drill sergeant."

"That's what he was."

"Oh, you know him?"

"I met him through my brother. My brother's a cop. So is my dad. I guess that's why I want to be one. Runs in the family. I went out with Duncan a couple times but he wanted more than dinner and a movie. I didn't. Besides, he's a little too old for me. I broke it off." She extended a hand "I'm Mimi Trent."

"George Evans." He took her hand. "I think he still has a thing for you. He looked right at me when he spouted that boy-meet-girl stuff."

Mimi's brow furrowed. "He can be pretty vindictive. He didn't take it very well when I turned him down. Just don't give him any reason in class to give you a hard time."

"Some guys think they're God's gift to women. I can go out to dinner and a movie with a girl and have a good time without expecting anything more."

"Are you asking me for a date?"

George's face crimsoned. "Yeah, I guess I am."

"Well, right now I want to concentrate on getting a good start in school. But ask me again in a week or so. Okay?"

They finished lunch and returned to the classroom, but for the rest of the afternoon George found it hard to keep his mind on lessons.

At the end of the day as he prepared to leave, Sgt. Duncan intercepted him. "I want to give you a little advice, Evans. This is going to be a tough course, and if you expect to get through it you don't want any distractions."

George felt his anger slowly rising. "Are you suggesting I not be friendly with Mimi?"

"Hey, I'm not threatening you or anything. I just want to give you some friendly advice."

"Yeah, thanks. I'll think about it."

DEATH TAKES A HONEYMOON
CHAPTER EIGHTEEN

Erin O'Neal had just entered the Wayland Corporation building and headed for the Personnel Office when Roger Mangum called to her from down the hall. "Hi, stranger, what're you doing here?"

She walked toward him. "I'm looking for a job."

"Well, come along with me." He took her elbow. "I'll introduce you to the boss."

"I've already met Mister Wayland. He was Best Man at Nora's wedding."

Roger's face fell. "Oh." He paused. "I wasn't invited to the wedding."

"Nora treated you really shabbily, Roger, but that shouldn't stop you and me from being friends."

"Of course not. Come on, let's go see Mister Wayland."

They proceeded to Matthew Wayland's office and walked through the open door. "Look who's here, Mister Wayland," Roger grinned.

Wayland stood up, smiling broadly, and extended a hand. "Hello, Erin, what a pleasant surprise. It's not every day that a beautiful young woman walks into my office. Sit down. Sit down."

"Erin is looking for a job, Mister Wayland," Roger said. "I'm late for a meeting so I'll leave her with you." He left the office.

For a long moment Wayland studied Erin, a bemused smile on his face. "What kind of job are you looking for, Erin? I think I can get you on the Caribbean Lady where you can meet a rich husband."

Erin pursed her lips. "That's not what I want. I want a job with a future, where I can work my way up and be somebody in the business world. I have no intention of having a man take care of me."

"Well, Erin, we do have an opening for a trainee in Planning and Expediting. You would be working under Roger." His eyes twinkled. "I mean that figuratively, of course."

"I think I'd like that, Mister Wayland. When can I start?"

"Go to the Personnel Office, Erin. I'll call them. They'll take care of you." He pressed her hand between his two. "Welcome to Wayland Construction."

I've got a foot in the door, Erin mused as she left the office, *now let's see if I can make Roger forget Nora.*

****

A wave of excitement swept through the offices of Wayland Construction as the rumor spread. Matthew Wayland called a meeting of his key personnel.

"People," he began, "what you have heard is true. We've landed a really big contract to build barracks at a NATO base in Turkey." He waited for the applause to die down before continuing. "I'm making Roger Mangum on-site Project Manager. We'll use mostly native labor but we'll send a core group of skilled workers." He pointed at Caleb Mangum and Jose Garcia. "I want you two to each pick eight to ten good men who will be willing to go there and stay until the job is completed. That could mean six months to a year away from home." He paused for effect. "There will be big bonuses for everybody."

The room erupted in a babble of excited voices. Wayland smiled. "I can see that you are all enthusiastic about this project. The construction crew will be flying out in about ten days. Everybody in the organization will have plenty to do to get ready so get hopping."

Jean Wayland had sat quietly at the back of the room as her father spoke, but as Roger started to leave she grasped his arm firmly. "I don't want you away from me for that long, Roger. We're getting married and I'm going with you."

Roger tensed.

"Don't you want to marry me?" she demanded.

"Yeah, I guess so. But I thought we would wait a little while." Her voice rose. "Well, I don't want to wait."

****

At the church, Roger Mangum pumped his friend's hand vigorously. "Thanks for standing up for me, George. My dad bowed out of the job. I know it was short notice and that you have a full schedule at the Police Academy, but Jean and I made a snap decision to marry. I hope I can return the favor and stand up for you some day."

George laughed. "What happened? Did you knock her up?"

"Nothing like that. The company got a contract to build barracks at a NATO base in Turkey, and the boss is sending me to head the operation. Jean and I have been dating and she wants to go with me. Out of the blue she suggested we get married." He paused. "I'm moving up in the company, George. I'm going to be a partner, now. Jean's father is giving me a share of the business as a wedding present."

George slapped Roger on the back. "Congratulations, buddy, and you might be able to return the favor sooner than you think."

"You got somebody in mind?"

"Yeah. I'm dating a girl at the Academy. Her name is Mimi. We get along great and we have been talking about marrying after we graduate." He gave a nervous laugh. "I always thought it would be you and Nora getting married."

Roger's face hardened. "She couldn't wait for me to make something of myself. She didn't even invite you and me to her wedding when she married that rich guy."

An organ began playing in the main hall. George placed a hand on his friend's shoulder. "We'd better get out there. You don't want to keep your bride waiting."

DEATH TAKES A HONEYMOON

As the happy couple exchanged vows, a young woman sat alone in the back row, a wide-brimmed hat covering her face. *Well, Roger, Nora thought, you've tasted champagne. Now I wonder if you'll be satisfied with jug wine.* She jumped up and ran from the chapel as the newlyweds turned and began the recessional.

Jean gripped Roger's elbow. "Wasn't that Nora?" she whispered.

A faint frown creased Roger's forehead. "I think so, but I certainly didn't invite her."

Forcing smiles, they ran the gauntlet of well-wishers blowing soap bubbles, paused long enough for Jean to toss her bridal bouquet into the air, then dashed for a waiting limousine.

Inside the car Jean kicked off her shoes, removed her headpiece and leaned back against the cushions, eyes closed. Abruptly she burst out "Roger, would you have married me if Nora had not already married someone else?"

He cradled her in his arms and kissed her gently. "Darling, I married you because I love you. Whatever there was between Nora and me ended when she dumped me as soon as I went to work for your father. You and I are going to have a good life together and we're not going to let Nora, or any memory of her, intrude into it. She's really a cold, calculating, ambitious woman."

Jean remained silent for a long moment before replying, almost in a whisper, "You say that you're over her, but is she over you?" She sat up suddenly and removed his arms from around her. "You know, Roger, you might have underestimated me. I wanted you in high school but Nora stood in the way so I had to get rid of her." She smiled smugly."You didn't bring a very high price. Dad bought her off for a pittance."

Roger bristled. "Your father paid Nora to dump me?"

"Yes, and I suspect he bought you, too. That was a pretty nice piece of company stock he gave you for marrying me."

Roger became rattled. "I....he..." He threw his arms around

her. "I married you because I love you."

She wriggled free and her voice rose. "Get one thing straight, Roger. Dad gave you a small interest in the business, but when my father dies I'll own the business, and according to the doctors his heart could quit at any time. The company retains the right to repurchase the stock he gave you, and you could be out in the cold." She looked at Roger cooly. "Do I make myself clear, my dear husband?"

Roger stiffened. *Damn! This is one side of Jean I never suspected. Is she as cold and calculating as Nora is?*

Nora ran from the chapel, rounded the building and leaped into her Mercedes convertible. Tires squealing, she roared out of the parking lot. She quickly settled down, blended into traffic, and drove to the Patarkis Airways Building.

"Where the hell have you been?" Victor shouted as she entered his office. "You know you have to pick Theodore up at the airport."

She stopped short and glared at him. "I'm your wife, Victor, not your slave. You can have a limo pick him up. His plane doesn't arrive for a couple hours, anyway. And it's none of your damned business where I've been."

"Theodore is family. Someone from family has to meet him and I can't get away right now." He grabbed some papers from his desk and waved them in her face. "Look at these credit card statements. You've been spending money like it's water. This extravagance has got to stop."

She snatched the bills from him, threw them to the floor and stomped on them. "I buy things I need, that's all. Victor, I gave up a lot marrying a much older man. You have to make it up to me in other ways." She stormed out of the office.

DEATH TAKES A HONEYMOON

At the airport Nora stood outside Customs and Immigration holding a sign reading "Patarkis." A grinning young man approached. "Hi, I'm Theodore Patarkis. My friends call me Ted. You must be my mother."

Nora's eyes flashed. "I am not your mother, Theodore, I'm your father's wife."

"Well, the old boy really knows how to pick them."

She started to walk away. "The baggage pickup is one level down."

"I'm traveling light. All I have is this carry-on bag. I keep clothes at the old man's place."

"Then follow me. My car is in the parking garage."

When they reached Nora's convertible Theodore let out a low whistle. "The old boy has as sharp a taste in wheels as he has in women."

"This is my car," Nora snapped. "Your father had nothing to do with selecting it."

Silence prevailed as they exited the parking garage, stopped to pay the parking fee, and left the airport. But as they headed down the highway, Theodore began rhythmically tapping on his knee and singing an old sea ditty. "Tell me pretty maiden, are there any more at home like you?"

Nora managed a tight smile. "I have a younger sister, but she is very discriminating in her choice of men. She wouldn't be interested in you."

He roared with laughter. "Truce, Nora! Truce! We'll be living under the same roof while I'm here so we might as well be civil to each other."

"All right, truce – Ted." She glanced at him sharply. "You're married. Don't tell me you inherited your father's roving eye."

"I won't be married much longer. Lydia and I are getting a divorce. But I'm nothing like my father in that way. I have never cheated on my wife."

"What do you mean by that?"

Ted hesitated for a long moment. "Is he still seeing Sherry Lord?"

"You know about Sherry?"

"She and my father were having an affair before my mother -- died."

They drove in silence for a few minutes before Nora spoke again. "You seem more like an American than a Greek."

"That's because I am. My mother was American and I was born and raised in Florida. I hold dual Greek and American citizenship."

"But you prefer to live on Samos?"

He laughed "That's not a matter of choice. The villa on Samos belonged to my grandfather. After he died my father inherited it. We went there often for vacations."

"Your mother and father were on vacation there when she was killed in the accident?"

"I was in college here and didn't go with them that time. After I graduated my father put me in charge of the family's European interests and I went to live on Samos. That's where I met Lydia. She's the daughter of Demetrius and Eleni."

Nora gasped. "I met Demetrius and Eleni but I was never told that you married their daughter!"

"Lydia was wild and exciting and I fell in love with her. It was not until after we were married that I found that she was addicted to drugs and alcohol. She's getting treatment now but we have agreed on an amicable divorce."

"How long will you be here?" Nora asked.

"Just a few days. There's an important meeting of all the directors of my father's many business enterprises and he said it was important that I attend."

DEATH TAKES A HONEYMOON

There was no further mention of Sherry Lord as they drove to the Star Island estate.

****

After the brief honeymoon at a local hotel, Roger and Jean took a taxi to a small commercial airport where they found a group of Wayland workers milling around a chartered plane sitting on the tarmac. Roger, still shaken from the acrimonious confrontation with Jean after the wedding, and the chilling realization the girl he married was not the meek little lamb he had thought her to be, eyed the plane. "Patarkis Airways! That's the name of the man Nora married."

Jean smiled sweetly. "Oh, yes. Victor Patarkis and Dad are good friends. Dad got Nora a job on Victor's cruise ship. That's where she met Victor. Come on, Roger, forget Nora. She's history. She's out of our lives and we'll never let her back in."

From the crowd of workmen Caleb Mangum called "Hi, son, sorry I couldn't make your wedding. I had to put my work crew together."

DEATH TAKES A HONEYMOON

CHAPTER NINETEEN

Graduation Day at the Police Academy finally arrived, and despite being constantly harasseed by their principal instructor, George and Mimi both were near the top of the class.

"What do you want to do after the ceremonies?" Mimi asked.

George grinned. "Well, after high school graduation a lot of the kids went to motels and..."

An impish smile lighted Mimi's face. "Let's do it one better. Let's fly out to Las Vegas and get married."

"You're kidding"

"I'm not kidding."

George's manner sobered. "That would really throw it into Sergeant Duncan's face."

"I'm not thinking about Duncan. George, you and I share the same interests. That's one of the reasons I love you. We have been talking about marriage. Let's do it."

He threw his arms around her. "Mimi, you're the greatest!"

On the plane to Vegas and in the taxi to the wedding chapel, George fidgeted nervously.

"Not getting cold feet are you, George, " Mimi asked.

"No. No."

The ceremony at the chapel was cold and scripted. "By the authority granted me by the State of Nevada I pronounce you husband and wife. You may kiss the bride." Money changed hands. The minister called "Next."

The newlyweds went immediately to a reserved hotel room. As they removed their clothes George hesitated. "Mimi, I've never made love to a girl before. I'm - - inexperienced."

DEATH TAKES A HONEYMOON

She gently took his hand and led him to the bed. "You don't have to be experienced." *No, my love, you don't have to be experienced, but I know from class that you're a fast learner. And I can be a very good teacher.*

Pearl Evans met George and Mimi at the airport when they returned from Las Vegas. "I've arranged a little reception for you lovebirds," she told them, "nothing fancy, just families and a few of your friends from high school and the academy. They'll be there when we get home."

A chorus of congratulations greeted the newlyweds as they entered the house. Sgt. Duncan, a sheepish grin on his face and a hand extended, was the first to approach them. "I know I was a little rough on you kids in class but that's my job. I gotta make tough cops out of raw recruits. I did good with you two. You gonna be good cops."

"Yeah, sure," George replied stiffly, "no hard feelings."

Duncan grabbed Mimi and planted a firm kiss on her lips. He turned to George. "Take good care of this gal. She's the best."

Mimi's father came over and shook George's hand. "Welcome to the family, son, and to the force."

The party had been in progress only a short while when a knock sounded on the door. Pearl Evans answered it and broke into a welcoming smile. "Come in, Nora, I was hoping you could make it."

CHAPTER TWENTY

"I hate this place," Jean screamed at Roger. "I feel like a prisoner. I can't leave the base alone, and I have no friends. Oh, sure, there are some military wives here but we have nothing in common. I never should have come here. I want to go home."

Roger tried to calm her. "The job's almost done. Just a few more finishing touches and some cleanup work and we can leave."

"Don't give me that bull. I heard you telling the men that we might get another contract here."

The telephone rang and Roger answered it. His face drained of color. "Yes, I'll tell her." He went over to Jean and took her in his arms. "Terrible news, darling. Your father just died of a heart attack."

She pulled free and threw herself onto a sofa, sobbing hysterically.

Roger quietly left the room and hurried to where his crew was working on the last barracks building. He beckoned to his father and Jose Garcia and they came over to him.

"Mister Wayland just died," he told them solemnly, "and I have to leave immediately to take Jean home. I'm counting on you two to finish the job. There's only about three week's work left to be done. When you're ready to leave I'll send a Patarkis plane to take you and your crews back to the States. Clean up the work sites and load all of our equipment aboard the plane." He repeated "I'm counting on you."

Caleb Mangum grasped Roger's hand. "We won't let you down, son."

The next morning Caleb drove Roger and Jean to a commercial airport and saw them off. He then went into a lounge, sat at the bar and ordered a drink. A swarthy man came in and took a seat next to him. The newcomer called out a few words in Turkish and the bartender brought him a beer. The man sipped from the mug for a few minutes and then turned to Caleb. "You work for a company doing work at the military airfield, no?"

Caleb eyed the man suspiciously. "Yeah, what of it?"

"You finish the job and go home in few days, no? In fact, soon a plane comes to take you to Miami."

"You seem to know an awful lot about my business. What's it to you?"

The man shrugged. "I have something I want to send to the United States. Because of Turkish government regulations I can't send it by commercial carrier. I can make it worthwhile for you to take the crate on the chartered plane."

"Hey, I'm not getting mixed up in narcotics smuggling."

"No narcotics are involved. Come with me to my car and let me show you something."

He threw some currency on the bar and Caleb followed him to the parking lot.

The Turk opened the trunk of his car and removed the lid from a small wooden crate, revealing a ceramic urn nested in straw.

"This is very old, maybe two thousand, three thousand years. My government prohibits the removal of such antiquities from the country. I can get a lot of money for it in America."

Caleb's eyes narrowed. "So you want me to smuggle it into the States? How could I get it past Customs? And what's in it for me?"

"You will pass it through American Customs as a souvenir you bought at a bazaar. Someone will meet you and take it from you, and give you one thousand dollars."

Caleb stroked his chin. "What's to keep me from running off with it?" The man gave him an evil smile. "You won't. You will be watched."

"Well, I guess I could do it. But we won't be leaving here for several weeks."

They transferred the urn to Caleb's car. "Be very careful with it," the Turk warned. "It is fragile."

When Caleb got back to the air base he placed the crate in the equipment storage building.

"Whatcha got there, Caleb?" Jose asked.

Caleb shrugged. "Just a souvenir I picked up at a bazaar."

CHAPTER TWENTY-ONE

"Matthew Wayland was my best friend and we're going to his viewing," Victor stormed.

"I'm not feeling well, Victor," Nora answered. *That uppity Jean Wayland will be there acting like queen of the ball - - and Roger will be there.*

"Well, I'm going and you're going, too. What will people think if you're not with me? Get dressed."

A steady stream of friends and business associates came to pay final respects to the amiable and highly respected industrialist. Serenely, Jean Wayland greeted each one while Roger stood by her side, uncertain as to his role. Jean's composure faltered for only a split second when she saw Victor and Nora approaching.

Victor gave her a quick hug. "Your father was a dear friend. I shall miss him."

Nora managed a "Sorry about your dad, Jean."

The arrival of George and Mimi ended the awkward moment of silence that followed. George hugged Jean. "I didn't know your father but I know how close you two were. I'm sure you'll miss him terribly."

He took Roger's hand. "I want you and Jean to meet my wife, Mimi. I'm sorry we couldn't wait for you to return from Turkey to be my Best Man." He paused. "Nora has already met her." He turned to Victor. "You don't remember me, do you Mister Patarkis?"

Victor studied him for a moment. "Oh, yes. You're the limo driver."

"I'm a police officer now, and so is Mimi." He looked back at Roger. "You know, Roger, this is the first time since the Senior Prom

DEATH TAKES A HONEYMOON

that you, Jean, Nora and I have all been together."

Jean glared at Nora. "That's not exactly true, is it Nora? You were at the church when Roger and I got married."

Erin O'Neal's appearance at that moment defused a potentially explosive situation. "I'll miss your dad, Jean. He was a wonderful boss." Then to Roger."Thanks again for getting me the job with Wayland Construction. I really love it."

Jean's eyes narrowed. *He got Nora's sister a job. I wonder if he is seeing Nora, too. Well, I own the company now and I'll decide whether Erin keeps that job.*

As more friends approached she quickly resumed the role of bereaved daughter.

Victor left the group to go stand by Matthew Wayland's coffin, but his thoughts were not entirely on his deceased friend. *Nora went to Roger's wedding, and she has met George's wife. What else is she doing behind my back?*

****

In the weeks following his return from Turkey, Roger worked tirelessly to fill the shoes of the late Matthew Wayland. He did not find the task an easy one; his father-in-law had kept a tight rein on the operation of the business and had delegated few responsibilities to subordinates. Jean chafed at his lack of attention to her.

"Where have you been?" she demanded when he returned home late one evening. "You know I wanted to go out."

"Some important work had to be finished. You know we're trying to do two big projects at the same time -- the job in Turkey and the Wayland Towers condo. I stayed late at the office."

"I called your office and got no answer."

Roger heaved a deep sigh. "Jean, I've told you before that I don't answer the phone after business hours. It rings a lot and callers would interrupt my work."

DEATH TAKES A HONEYMOON

"Have you been seeing Nora O'Neal behind my back?" she demanded.

He took a sharp breath. "Can't you forget about Nora? I have. What there was between us ended a long time ago."

"You got a job for her sister, Erin," Jean accused.

"Erin came to the office looking for a job. I happened to run into her in the hallway and took her to see your dad. I didn't wait around to see if he hired her. Now if you still want to go out I'll take a quick shower and be ready in a few minutes."

"Don't bother!" She stormed out of the room.

The next day Jean stood before a door with a translucent panel lettered NICOLAS SAVAGE, PRIVATE INVESTIGATOR. She hesitated a moment getting up her courage, then rapped lightly on the panel.

"It's open," a voice from inside called.

She entered the office and made a quick evaluation. Bare vinyl tile floor in need of a shine. A row of file cabinets along one wall. Two leather-covered chairs. A window overlooking downtown Miami. In front of the window a cluttered desk, a tan-faced man with tousled sand-colored hair sitting behind it. "I'm Jean Wayland Mangum. I called this morning for an appointment."

He lifted his six-foot-two frame from his chair and extended a hand. "I'm Nick Savage. Have a seat and tell me what I can do for you."

She shook his hand and then sat nervously on the edge of a chair facing him. "I want someone watched."

"Your husband?"

Jean lifted her eyebrows. "How did you know it's my husband?"

"When a woman hires a PI it's almost always her husband she wants checked on. Is yours playing around?"

DEATH TAKES A HONEYMOON

"That's what I want to find out. He's been acting -- secretive."

"So how much surveillance do you want?"

"I want to know everywhere he goes from the time he arrives at his office in the morning until he gets home at night."

"That could be expensive. I get five hundred per day plus expenses."

Jean eyed him suspiciously. "What kind of expenses?"

He shrugged. "Sometimes I have to buy information. Like from a hotel desk clerk or a cabbie. Sometimes I have to rent a motel room to keep an eye on a guy who also has rented a motel room."

"Well, whatever it costs. My husband is Roger Mangum. His office is in the Wayland Building."

Savage glanced at her sharply. "You're Matthew Wayland's daughter, aren't you?"

"You knew my father?"

"Yeah. Great guy. I did work for him from time to time. I was sorry to hear that he died."

Jean handed him a photograph. "This is a picture of Roger. He gets to the office around seven in the morning and usually leaves around six in the evening. He drives a white Taurus station wagon."

"Phew! That's long working hours. What is he, a workaholic?"

"Since my father died Roger has been pretty much running the company. We just got back from Turkey where we spent almost a year on a construction project. He has a lot of catching up to do on the operations."

"I can't see where he would find time to mess around. Do you suspect he's seeing anyone in particular?"

She didn't answer but hurriedly wrote out a check and handed it to him. "Here's a five thousand dollar retainer. You just keep an eye on him." She reached into her purse and pulled out a card. "Here is my private telephone number. You can reach me there or leave a message on my answering machine." As she started to leave the office she looked back over her shoulder. "You will be discreet won't you Mister Savage?"

"It's Nick, Jean."

She gave a little wave and left. *Nick Savage. There's a man who could really turn me* on.

DEATH TAKES A HONEYMOON

CHAPTER TWENTY-TWO

At his office Victor Patarkis leafed through some bills on his desk. "Come here, Mabel," he called to his secretary. She entered his office. He pointed to a telephone bill. "I make calls to Theodore at his office, but who do we call at this other number on Samos?"

She looked at the bill. "Oh, that's your son's cellphone number."

His eyes narrowed. "I never call him at that number."

Mabel shrugged. "Maybe your wife makes the calls."

The telephone on Victor's desk rang and the secretary picked it up. "Patarkis Airlines. How may I help you?" She quickly handed the phone to Victor. "It's the pilot of the plane sent to pick up the Wayland people. He sounds excited."

Victor took the phone. "Yes?" He listened for a moment and then exploded. "Those bastards! Just sit tight and I'll get there as soon as I can. I know how to handle that band of thieves." He hung up and turned to Mabel. "Some contraband was found on the plane and the authorities have impounded it. Get me on the next available flight to Turkey."

While the secretary called a travel agency, Victor went to a safe and counted out a hundred 100-dollar bills. He placed the money in a brief case.

Mabel came back into the office. "There's a flight to Rome with a connecting flight to Ankara departing in four hours. I made a reservation for you."

Highly agitated, Victor hurried home to pack for the trip. When he entered the house he shouted at Nora. "Have you been telephoning Theodore?"

She glared at him. "Is there any reason I shouldn't? I'm trying to be friendly with your son."

His face contorted. "Did you have an affair with him when he was here?"

"No I didn't," she snapped, "but maybe I should have. You sure haven't been much good in bed lately. Maybe you've been spending it all on Sherry Lord."

Victor flew into a rage. "You would cuckold me with my own son?" He delivered a sharp slap to her face. Then another and another, harder.

She dropped to her knees, screaming. "Victor, you're hurting me."

"I should kill you, you bitch! You tricked me into marrying you and now you would dishonor me. I have to go on a business trip and when I get back I don't want to find you here. Get out." His voice rose."Get out." He bolted up the stairs, leaving Nora still kneeling on the floor.

After Victor left, Nora stumbled to a telephone and tapped in a number. "George," she moaned, "please come here. I need your help."

****

The police car screeched to a stop in front of the Star Island mansion. George and Mimi jumped out and ran toward the front entrance. A woman sat on the marble steps, her face buried in her hands.

"Is that you, Nora?" George called.

When the woman looked up, Mimi screamed "Oh my God, somebody's worked her over."

Nora's face was a mass of bloody welts.

George put his arms around Nora's shoulders. "What happened, Nora?"

DEATH TAKES A HONEYMOON

"Victor beat me."
"Where is he now?"
"He's gone."
George started to lift her up. "You're hurt. We have to get you to a hospital."
She pulled away. "Pictures, George, I need pictures. I've got Victor by the balls now. He'll tear up that damned pre-nup agreement or I'll put his ass in prison."
George turned to Mimi, his voice reflecting his exasperation. "Get the video camera from the car, honey." He looked back at Nora. "How did it happen?"
"Victor accused me of having an affair with his son. He found that I had made phone calls to Ted. Ted wants to come here and throw a surprise birthday party for his father. I was helping him set it up. That's all there was to it. Victor jumped to the wrong conclusion. He's got a really nasty temper. He lost it and slugged me. Over and over."
Mimi returned with the camera and began taking views of Nora's face from several angles.. When she finished, George again put his arms around Nora's shoulders. "We'd better get you to the hospital to have those bruises checked and to see if there's any internal damage."
"No! I don't want..." She suddenly went limp in his arms. He carried her to the patrol car. "You drive, Mimi," he ordered, "I'll hold her."

As the emergency room staff worked feverishly to revive Nora and attend to her injuries, a doctor approached George and Mimi. "I'm Doctor Gerard. This woman appears to have been brutalized. Do you know what happened?"
"She told us that her husband beat her."
The doctor's eyes narrowed. "She was conscious when you

85

found her?"

"Yes. She passed out as we were getting her to the patrol car."

"Isn't it standard police procedure to call for an ambulance in cases like this?"

George shifted his feet uneasily. "It was not an official police call. She's a friend of ours. We were off duty at home when she called for help."

Doctor Gerard looked at them sharply. "You two are married to each other?"

"Yes."

"You know that I'll have to make a full report to the authorities."

"I wish you wouldn't," George said.

"Why not? This is a most unusual situation, and I'm sure you know the law."

"She said she didn't want us to go after her husband, and she doesn't want any publicity."

"Well," the doctor turned away, "I have to file a report. The lady can use her own judgement as to whether she wants to bring charges against the person who did this to her."

Nora began to stir. "She's coming out of it," one of the nurses exclaimed.

George rushed over to the side of the gurney. Nora opened her eyes and looked around, confused. Slowly her eyes focused on George's face. "George," she murmured weakly, "where am I?"

"You're in the hospital emergency room. Mimi and I brought you here. Now just relax. You're going to be okay."

Dr. Gerard looked at her and then at the two police officers. "We're going to admit her for observation and treatment. You can see her tomorrow morning if you wish. Go over to the admissions clerk and give her what information you can on the patient. Meanwhile, you might want to start thinking about how you will explain your actions to your precinct captain."

Nora greeted them the next morning with a weak wave of her hand. Bandages concealed any expression that might have been on her face. Her voice was not much stronger than on the previous night.

"Thanks, George," she whispered. "I owe you big."

George walked over to her. "You remember Mimi being with me last night when we picked you up?"

"Vaguely. Last night is all a fog."

The two pulled up chairs and sat beside the bed. He looked into Nora's swollen eyes. "Nora, last night you told us that your husband beat you. Do you want to file charges against him?"

"No! No!" Nora's reply came in sharp gasps. "I can take care of Victor."

"Well, he messed your face up pretty bad. I spoke to the doctor before we came in. He wants to keep you here for a few days for observation. Some tests they took indicated some irregularity not attributed to the injuries. When you're ready to leave the hospital we'll pick you up and take you home."

"No!" Nora panicked. "I can't go back to Star Island. Victor would kill me."

Mimi took her hand. "Don't worry. We'll find a safe place for you."

Shortly after George and Mimi left, a nurse stuck her head in the door and called cheerfully "You have a visitor." She stepped aside and Roger entered the room.

Nora quickly covered her bandaged face with her hands. "I don't want you to see me like this."

He sat down beside her bed. "George told me what happened. Your husband must be a monster to do this to you. Are you going to leave him?"

"I can't. But I've got him where I want him. He'll do everything I ask now or I'll send him to prison."

"That's no way to live."

"No? Tell me, Roger, are you leading the kind of life you want?"

Roger sighed. "You know, you and I are more alike than you might think. You married for money and I married Jean because my career depended on it." He gave a mirthless laugh. "Maybe we both got what we deserved." He quickly added "But you didn't deserve to get beaten."

"You wish things had turned out differently?" Nora asked softly.

He stood up. "The nurse told me not to stay long and tire you. I'll always have - - feelings for you, Nora. If there's anything I can do for you just let me know."

So he still has 'feelings' for me, Nora thought after he left. She drifted off to sleep remembering the ecstasy of their time as young lovers.

****

Nick Savage telephoned Jean at her office. "Today your husband had lunch with a police officer. I got the badge number and will get his name for you."

"Don't bother. I think I know who he was. Where did Roger go after that?"

"Right after he left the cop he went to Memorial Hospital, to the room of a patient named Nora Patarkis. I got pictures of him with the cop and pictures of him going into the hospital room."

"Well, hold on to the photos. Forget about Roger for the time

DEATH TAKES A HONEYMOON

being. Find out why Nora is in the hospital, and when she's released keep her under surveillance."

CHAPTER TWENTY-THREE

A government car met Victor when he landed, and whisked him off to the office of a minor Turkish official. As he entered, a swarthy man looked up from a desk.

"Ah, Victor, it makes my heart happy that you could come so promptly."

"Yes," Victor replied dryly, "I'm sure it does. You set me up again, Ibrahim."

The man feigned a pained expression. "Victor, Victor. I am but a lowly public servant doing my job. Someone tried to smuggle a banned antiquity from my country to your country and I was so fortunate to detect it."

"Yes, you were so fortunate," Victor sneered. "How did you manage to get it on my plane?"

Ibrahim ignored the insinuation. "You brought the money?"

"Did I have an option?" Victor placed the stacks of currency on the desk. "Ten thousand as usual."

"But no, Victor. That is not enough The price has gone up. You know, inflation and all."

"You'll take it," Victor roared. "I'll go over your head even if it means my plane will be held here for weeks."

"You get paid well for bringing the American construction people here," Ibrahim shrugged. "Consider my fees a part of the cost of doing business."

The Turk picked the money up and put it into a briefcase. "The next time it will be more." He smiled and stuck out his hand. "Do return soon, Victor."

"There'll be no next time, Ibrahim," Victor snorted. "No plane of mine will ever fly into your jurisdiction again."

DEATH TAKES A HONEYMOON

Ibrahim shrugged."When you arrived at the airport I gave orders for your plane to be released. The crew and passengers are waiting for you. I will have a police escort take you to where the plane is being held."

Siren wailing, the police car sped up to the parked plane and braked to a stop. Victor got out and called to the pilot. "Ready to take off, Captain Daniels?"

Daniels snapped to attention. "Yes, sir. I've been ready."

As Victor started toward the plane a crazed man, waving a pistol and screaming in Turkish, bolted across the tarmac. He got off one shot before a fusillade of police bullets cut him down. Victor slumped to the pavement, mortally wounded. His life blood oozed out to blend with the blood of his assassin on the cold, grey concrete.

The pilot rushed over to Victor and felt for a pulse."He's dead," he called to the Wayland workers staring in horror. "Get him aboard and let's get the hell out of here."

"No!" a policeman shouted, " you cannot leave. There will be an inquiry."

"Screw the inquiry. We're taking off."

With Victor's body, and all of the workers aboard, the plane sped down the runway. Ignoring frantic warnings from the control tower, Captain Daniels lifted the plane off and it roared into the sky, narrowly avoiding a collision with an incoming flight.

Seated in the back of the plane, Caleb Mangum suddenly retched.

"Can't stand the sight of blood, Caleb?" Jose grinned.

Caleb continued to dry-heave violently. *Oh, God, what have I done? I got a man killed."*

CHAPTER TWENTY-FOUR

A nurse rushed into the hospital room and hastily hooked Nora to a monitor.

"What's that for," Nora demanded, "I'm being released this morning."

The nurse avoided her gaze. "Doctor's orders. He'll be in to see you in a few minutes."

Dr. Gerard entered the room, approached Nora's bed and gently took her hand. "I have some sad news, Mrs. Patarkis." He paused. "Your husband has met with a terrible misfortune." He paused again, struggling to find the right words. He looked at her compassionately. "Your husband is dead."

Nora bolted upright. "Oh, no! How could he do this to me? How could he do this to me?"

The doctor looked at her sharply. "Didn't you understand what I said? Madam, your husband is dead!"

****

In contrast to the outpouring of respect for Matthew Wayland, not many people showed up at the funeral home to honor Victor Patarkis. Though he had many business associates, he had few friends. He did have enemies. The news media reported that the man who killed him was a member of an extremist Turkish Cypriot organization that had a vendetta against the Patarkis family.

The few business associates who did come paid their respects and left immediately. George and Mimi were among the first of Nora's friends to arrive but had to leave early. "We both go on duty in about an hour," George explained.

Only Sherry Lord appeared to be genuinely grieved. As she

DEATH TAKES A HONEYMOON

hesitantly approached Nora and Ted Patarkis, standing with Erin O'Neal beside Victor's casket, Roger Mangum suddenly came in. He spotted Nora and hurried over. "I don't know what to say, Nora. You know how I felt about your husband."

Nora quickly turned to Ted. "Ted, this is Roger Mangum, a friend from high school days." Then to Roger. "Ted is Victor's son."

Roger took Ted's hand. "No offense to you, Ted, but I had no respect for your father." He released Ted's hand and pressed Nora's hand gently between his two. "I can stay only a moment. Jean is waiting for me to come home to dinner. I just want you to know that if there's anything I can do... " His voice trailed off.

"Thank's Roger," Nora replied. "I appreciate your coming."

As Roger turned to leave, Erin touched his elbow. "My car is in the shop and I came by cab. Could I trouble you to take me home?"

"No trouble at all, Erin. I go right past your neighborhood." They left together.

Sherry looked at Ted soberly. "I can understand how you feel about me. Your father was a very complex person but please believe that I did love him."

Through a widow's veil that concealed the scars on her face, Nora gave her a scornful glare. "If you loved him why did you encourage me to open my door to him on the Caribbean Lady?"

Sherry hesitated. "We need to talk, Nora. Let's go to where we can be alone. Will you excuse us, Ted?" Without waiting for his reply, she took Nora's elbow and guided her to a small anteroom. They entered and sat down.

For a long moment Sherry struggled to find words. "It was because I loved him that I did things for him. Victor had a lust for young women and it became my unhappy task to procure them for him. When I set you up with him I never dreamed he would marry you."

DEATH TAKES A HONEYMOON

She took a tissue from a dispenser on a lamp table and dabbed at her eyes. "I was about your age when I first met him. I was married and so was he but I fell in love with him. Soon afterwards he and his wife went to Greece on vacation and she was killed in an accident there."

"Yes," Nora said, "he showed me where it happened. Do you think he had anything to do with the accident?"

Sherry looked down at the floor. "I don't like to think he did. He said he was in the car with her but was thrown free. There were no witnesses and there was no inquiry." She paused. "He had a lot of influence on the island. After Victor came back to Florida, my husband, Dick, had a tragic scuba diving accident. If Dick had died, Victor and I would have been free to marry. But Dick didn't die right away. He remained in a coma for ten years. So I became Victor's mistress and his procurer."

"Well," Nora sniffed, "you did me no favor setting me up with him. My life has been a living hell. After I fell down a staircase on Samos and lost the baby, he grew cold and distant. I stayed with him because a pre-nup agreement I signed would have given me almost nothing if I left him." She gave a hollow laugh. "Now that he's dead I'll still get nothing. I don't know where I'll go or what I'll do."

"You're a smart girl, Nora. I'm sure you'll get along just fine wherever you go." Sherry smiled wistfully. "I'm going back to the Caribbean Lady. Maybe some day Mister Right will knock on the door to my cabin."

When Nora emerged from the anteroom she saw only Ted Patarkis standing alone. He gave her a wan smile. "It's just you and me now, Mother."

"Please, Ted," Nora answered wearily, "Don't call me Mother."

He put an arm around her shoulders. "I'd rather call you my

wife."

She gave him a sharp glance. "Take me home, Ted."

****

Jean found a message on her answering machine the next morning. "Nick Savage, Jean. You know about Victor Patarkis being killed, don't you? Nora Patarkis was released from the hospital and was at his viewing last night. Roger came to the viewing and he left there with a young woman he dropped off at an address I checked to be the home of an O'Neal family."

CHAPTER TWENTY-FIVE

With the death of Victor Patarkis, the Greek tycoons's house of cards collapsed. While he owned a number of businesses, all were heavily mortgaged. Like a pack of hungry wolves at the scent of a fallen deer, his creditors pounced greedily.

Nora had met Victor's attorney, Marcus Scales, but still felt a sense of foreboding when, nearly a month after Victor's death, Scales summoned her to his office. In the days following Victor's funeral, fears for her future had tormented her mind and she was not sure that she wanted, now, to know exactly what lay in store for her.

After leaving the hospital she had returned to Star Island. Ted Patarkis had come from Greece for his father's funeral and had remained to share the big house with her. While he was attentive to her, he did not repeat the suggestion made at the funeral chapel that she be his wife.

The receptionist greeted her with a sympathetic smile. "I'm sorry about your husband's death, Missus Patarkis." She turned and spoke into an intercom. "Missus Patarkis is here, Mister Scales."

"Send her in."

The lawyer met Nora halfway when she entered his office. "Come in, Nora. Too bad it took this sad occasion for us to meet again." Taking her hand, he guided her to his desk where he placed a chair for her. He then sat down across from her and lost no time in getting down to business.

"Victor named me his Personal Representative with authority to handle his estate when he passed on. You are not mentioned in his Will but the prenuptial agreement between you and Victor grants you five thousand dollars a month for as long as you remain un-remarried, and the court has given me permission to remit the first installment." His face sobered. "The estate is in terrible financial condition. I don't

DEATH TAKES A HONEYMOON

know how long there will be funds available to continue the payments. After all the costs of settling the estate are paid I don't think there will be much left for any of his heirs. And I'm afraid that you will have to vacate the Star Island place. Did you know that a foreclosure action had been filed on it before Victor's death?"

"No, Victor didn't tell me. He never discussed finances with me except to complain about my spending. But where will I go?. This amount will hardly more than pay the rent on a decent apartment."

Scales shrugged. "Then you will have to find something a little less decent. Believe me, Nora, I feel for you but you will not be able to live as extravagantly as you and Victor did."

"What about Victor's son?" Nora asked. "Will he be left out in the cold, too?"

The lawyer smiled. "A while back Victor transferred all of his European interests to Theodore. While he heavily mortgaged all of his other assets, he left these unencumbered. It is very apparent that he foresaw his financial collapse coming and put as many assets as he could beyond the reach of creditors. Young Mister Patarkis is a man of considerable wealth."

"How soon will I have to leave Star Island and what can I take with me? And what about my car?"

"You can take your personal effects and any gifts that Victor or others gave you. Your car is not listed in the inventory of the estate's assets so I assume it is registered in your name." He paused. "You cannot be forcibly evicted from the property until after the foreclosure sale but I would suggest that you begin making plans as quickly as possible."

Nora picked up the check from the desk and stood up to leave. "I won't give you any trouble, Mister Scales."

Scales took her hand. "Good luck, Nora. Keep me advised as to where I can reach you."

DEATH TAKES A HONEYMOON

As Nora took the elevator down she thought *So 'young Mister Patarkis is a man of considerable wealth'. Hmm.*
She went to the parking lot and got into her Mercedes convertible. *Well, at least the car is still mine. Now let me see what else I can salvage from a miserable marriage..*

When she reached home she met Ted coming out the door. He had a briefcase in one hand and was pulling a suitcase behind."I have to make a quick trip to New York to see some bankers who might help save some of Dad's enterprises. Don't do anything rash while I'm away." He suddenly dropped the luggage and wrapped his arms around her. He planted a passionate kiss on her lips.
She pushed him away gently. "Please Ted..."
"I haven't been able to get you off my mind since that first day we met at the airport, Nora. I planned the birthday party for my dad to have an excuse to see you again. It's been pure torture being in the same house with you these past weeks and not taking you into my arms. But I had to show some respect for my father's memory." He paused. " I really meant what I said at the funeral home."
"Please, Ted. It's too early to even have such thoughts. What would people say?"
"I don't give a damn what people think. I want you, Nora. We could slip off to some out-of-the way town and get married and nobody would even know. We could have a wonderful life together on Samos." He glanced at his watch. "I have to run to catch my flight. Please be ready to say 'yes' when I get back." He kissed her again and dashed for his car.
Nora watched until his car disappeared. *What kind of proposal was that? But better than Victor's "I've decided to make you my wife."*
She turned and slowly walked into the empty house. *Wow, this place is spooky with everybody gone.* The servants had all been

let go, the administrators of Victor's estate conserving what cash remained. *Worried about money to cover their fees,* Nora thought wryly.

She walked out onto the patio. The swimming pool was already becoming murky from lack of chemicals. *I couldn't even afford to keep the grass cut* she mused, looking out at once-manicured lawns now badly in need of mowing.

With a shrug she went back into the house, climbed the stairs to her bedroom. She kicked off her shoes, lay down on her bed and looked up at the reflected image in the mirrored ceiling. "Well, Nora O'Neal Patarkis," she said out loud, "do you think you would be happy living on Samos?" She saw her reflection nod "yes". *And I wouldn't even have to change the name on my personal stationery or the initials on my handkerchiefs.*
She picked up her telephone and tapped in a number. A recorded message answered. "This is the Evans residence. We can't take your call at this time but at the sound of the tone please leave a message and we will get back to you."

"George, this is Nora. I have to leave Star Island. Do you know where I might find a decent apartment? I don't want to stay here one night longer than I have to."

CHAPTER TWENTY-SIX

Nora was having breakfast the next morning when George called. He sounded excited.

"I've found a place for you. The Wayland Company is completing a high-rise condo and they have furnished several model apartments. I talked to Roger and he said that you could stay in one of them until you make a permanent arrangement. You might even consider buying one."

"No, George. I can't accept favors from Roger. Not after the way I've treated him. And as for buying there, forget it. The pre-nup agreement I signed when I married Victor leaves me practically destitute."

"Roger insisted on it." George paused. "He said to tell you that there are no strings attached. He will be there around eleven. At least go and talk to him. Do you know where it is?"

"Yes. It's been heavily advertised. All right, I'll talk to him. Thanks, George. You and Mimi are just about the only friends I have now. Except for Erin, my family has practically disowned me."

"What about Victor's son? Don't you get along with him?"

"Yes, I get along with Ted."

"Well, let me know if you take Roger up on his offer." He hung up.

Yes, Nora mused, *what about Victor's son?*

Nora had trouble getting to sleep that night, agonizing over Roger's offer. *He said there are no strings attached, but I wonder. At the hospital he said that he still has feelings for me. Is this his attempt to get back with me? But he's married...* She finally drifted off.

DEATH TAKES A HONEYMOON

A perky salesperson greeted Nora when she arrived at the condo the next day. "Welcome to Wayland Towers, the ultimate residence for those who appreciate the finer things in life. I'm Cindy. Please let me show you around."

"Mister Mangum is expecting me. Oh, there he is over there."

Roger was giving instructions to a man in painter's coveralls. "Good morning, Nora," he called to her, "I'll be with you in a few minutes."

He finished his conversation with the worker and walked over to give Nora a quick hug. "Come on, I'll show you the apartment. It's on the next level up. There's an elevator but it's quicker to take the stairs."

A sweeping circular staircase led up from the lobby. *What is it about staircases?* Nora thought, *First the Queen's Staircase in Nassau and then the stone staircase leading up to the villa on Samos.* But to Roger she said "This place is fabulous, the staircase looks as if it belongs in an old Southern mansion."

Roger grinned. "That's the theme of Wayland Towers – Old South charm with up-to-the-minute modern convenience and safety."

"That's something I was concerned about," Nora said. "I see that the building is still being worked on. Is there anyone living here? Will I be safe?"

"Oh, don't worry. A few buyers have already moved in and there is a security guard on duty at night. Besides that, no one can get into the building, day or night, without a pass card. That is, when we're not holding open house. But come on, let me show you your new home."

He led the way up the stairs and to a door which he opened with a key. "This unit has a balcony overlooking the ocean. I think

DEATH TAKES A HONEYMOON

you'll like it here."

Nick Savage emerged from an elevator and turned toward them.

After Roger and Nora closed the door, a security guard eyed Nick..

"What are you doing up here, sir?"

"I'm thinking about buying a condo."

"Well, you'll have to go back down to the lobby and have one of the hospitality ladies show you around."

"I don't have time for a guided tour right now. I'll come back later."

Nick turned and hurried down the stairs. The guard followed a short distance behind and jotted down the license plate number of the car Nick got into.

Roger guided Nora into the apartment and closed the door.

"This is the living room, with the balcony overlooking the ocean." He pointed to the left. "On this side is the kitchen and the guest bedroom and bath. You can fix your own meals if you want to but there are several good restaurants within walking distance." With a nod of his head he pointed. "On the other side is the master bedroom with a private bath."

They entered the bedroom. Roger went over and patted the bed. "Nice soft mattress, Nora," he grinned.

"No, Roger," Nora said firmly.

"No what?"

"No to whatever you're thinking."

He put his arms around her. "This is the kind of place I always dreamed you and I would share."

"Please, Roger, you told George there were no strings

attached."

"Alright, no strings, but I can always hope."

"Don't talk like that. I've just gone through the shock of losing a husband..."

"Shock?" he interrupted her. "I would say it's more of a relief. Or have you forgotten that he beat you?"

Nora turned toward the door. "I could never afford this place and I'm not going to accept charity. We can't go back to where we were, Roger. And have you forgotten that you are married?"

"Jean and I haven't been getting along well lately."

"No?" Nora scoffed. "Now isn't that interesting. Jug wine is not so tasty, is it?

He bristled. "What do you mean by that crack?"

"Oh, never mind. But don't think for a minute she would give you a divorce, and even if she did she would clean you. I've grown accustomed to the champagne life, Roger, and I'm not going to give it up. Thanks for your offer of this condo, whatever your motive, but I can't accept it." She left, leaving him standing alone.

Later that day the security guard called Roger's office. "There was a suspicious-looking man hanging around the building this morning, Mister Mangum. I got his license number and a buddy of mine at the DMV checked it out. The car belongs to a PI by the name of Nick Savage."

Roger stiffened. *Am I being watched or is Nora? M*aybe *he was keeping an eye on one of the new residents.* "Let me know if you see him again," he told the guard. "Thanks for calling."

CHAPTER TWENTY-SEVEN

Nora left Wayland Towers and drove back to Star Island. Upon entering the house she went to a telephone and tapped in George and Mimi's number. To her surprise, Mimi answered.

"Oh, hi, Mimi, this is Nora. I didn't expect to find you home. Is George there?"

"No, he's on duty. This is my day off. Is anything wrong?"

"No. Just tell him I've decided to stay at the Star Island place until they throw me out."

"Will you be all right there alone?"

Nora gave a little laugh. "I could use some company. This place is getting kind of spooky."

Mimi remained silent for a moment. "Maybe George and I could spend nights with you. I'll ask him when he comes home."

"I wouldn't want to impose on you," Nora quickly demurred. She hesitated. "It really would be great of you, if it's not too much trouble."

"It wouldn't be any trouble for me. Let's see what George says."

I'll stay here until they throw me out. Or until Ted Patarkis takes me to Samos Nora mused after she hung up.

She glanced around the spacious living room that once throbbed to the sounds of lavish parties, and out onto the patio and pool area. *Well, you were terrific as a playboy mansion but you really blew it as a Cinderella castle.*

Nora was having lunch when George returned her call.

"Hi, Nora. I just talked to Mimi. You didn't take Roger up on his offer?"

"No, there were strings attached. Roger wanted to go back to where we were in high school. As I told Mimi, I'm staying here as long as I can."

"I'm sorry it didn't work out with Roger's offer. Do you still want company?"

"I sure do. Can you and Mimi come?"

"Yes, Mimi said she would like to feel what it's like living in a millionaire mansion."

"That would be great of you two to comfort a poor old widow. But I hope Mimi won't be disappointed; this place has seen better days." She paused. "Don't eat before you come. I still have a freezer full of steaks. I'll thaw some. You know how to broil them on a propane grill, don't you? I don't. I can bake potatoes, though, and I picked up some fresh green salad on my way home."

George laughed. "It'll be fun. We'll be there around six. Have those potatoes in the oven."

After ending the call Nora thought *In high school I didn't realize what a good friend George could be.*

As they ate dinner that night, Nora suddenly burst out "I'm going to marry Ted Patarkis."

George looked up in surprise. "Are you sure that's what you want? Don't you think you should wait a while before making such an important decision?"

"Yes," Mimi agreed, "your life is in a turmoil right now and you might not be thinking very clearly. You should not rush into anything."

"Ted says he's been crazy about me since we first met, and I do like him. He probably won't inherit much from his father but Victor's lawyer told me that Ted is wealthy in his own right."

"Having money doesn't always bring happiness," George said. "I think you have already learned that." He threw an admiring glance at Mimi. "I found happiness with the greatest girl in the world, and we're not exactly rolling in dough."

Mimi gave him a quick hug and turned to Nora. "Where will you live? Do you think Ted might save this place?"

"Ted wants to take me to Samos. He has a gorgeous villa on the island. I really fell in love with it during the short time Victor and I were there together."

"But to be so far from family and friends, in a land where you don't speak the language," Mimi paused. "Do you think you could handle it?"

Nora smiled. "I'd miss you guys. My father opposed my marriage to Victor and things have been strained between us since. I don't think he will take kindly to my marrying Ted. Erin will be pleased though. She has a thing for Roger, and with me out of the picture she'll feel she has a better shot at him."

George raised his eyebrows. "Erin wants Roger? But he's married."

"She's had a crush on him since she was a teenager. Roger told me this morning that he and Jean are not getting along. I'm pretty sure he would like to get out of the marriage. I'm also sure that if Jean gave him a divorce she would see to it that he ended up in the financial gutter."

"There you go thinking money again, Nora," Mimi admonished her. "Erin might not view riches the way you do."

"Well," Nora replied, "I AM going to marry Ted."

CHAPTER TWENTY-EIGHT

The morning after Nick followed Nora to Wayland Towers he called Jean. "Are you busy, Jean?"

"Not particularly. What's up?"

"Can you come to my office? I have something very interesting to show you."

"I'll come right over." *Yeah, I could show that handsome hunk something interesting, too*

Nick met Jean at the door when she arrived at his office. "Come on in, Jean, and see what you're getting for your money." He led her to his desk and picked up a stack of photographs. "These are pictures I have taken since the first day of surveillance of Roger and Nora." He placed one on the desk. "This is the one of him meeting with the cop I told you about."

"That's George Evans, just as I thought."

He took more pictures from the stack. "Here is Roger visiting Nora at the hospital, and here he is going to the viewing of Nora's dead husband." He set another picture down. "Here is Roger leaving the funeral chapel with a young woman."

"That's Erin O'Neal, Nora's sister."

"It gets better, Jean. This is a picture taken yesterday morning of Nora going into Wayland Towers. And here's the jackpot." With a flourish he tossed the last photo on his desk. "Here Roger and Nora enter one of the units together."

"That bastard!" Jean exclaimed, "In our own building! How long did they stay there?"

"A security guard got suspicious so I had to leave in a hurry. Her car was still in the parking lot." He paused. "There's no doubt that your husband is cheating on you. You should get even."

DEATH TAKES A HONEYMOON

"How?"

Nick placed his lips close to hers. "Does this give you an idea?" He kissed her gently.

A wild wave of primeval passion swept through Jean's body. She kissed him back fervently. "Where?" she breathed.

"The upper floors of this building is a hotel. I have a room there."

She grabbed his hand. "Let's go."

Later as they lay beside each other she teased. "Will the cost of this room be charged to my account?"

He laughed. "No, everything today is on me. The pleasure was all mine."

"Not entirely yours," she whispered. She pressed her body against his and began stimulating him with her fingers.

"Hey," he murmured, "shouldn't I be watching Nora?"

She rolled over on top of him. "I want you to continue to keep an eye on Nora, but not right now."

CHAPTER TWENTY-NINE

George and Mimi continued to spend nights with Nora. Ted called frequently from New York. "Bankers here are reluctant to make any commitment to try to save any of my father's financial interests," he told Nora. "I think they are lying back in the hope of picking them up at bargain-basement prices. Thank goodness he put the European assets in my name. We won't ever have to worry about money. You are going to marry me, aren't you?"

Nora avoided giving him a definite answer. "We'll talk about it when you get back."

A few days later Nora told George and Mimi at breakfast. "Ted is coming home today."

Mimi laughed. "Then you won't want us hanging around."

"I guess he will want some privacy. Hey, you guys have been really great company and I'll never forget what you've done for me."

Ted returned home in the early evening. He swept Nora into his arms. "I didn't have any luck in New York but it really doesn't matter as long as I have you."

She wriggled free and stepped back. "Ted, I've decided to make you my husband."

His mouth dropped open. "What?"

"When I suggested to your father that we get married he said 'I've decided to make you my wife'. Now you have suggested that you and I…"

He grabbed her again and kissed her passionately. "I didn't suggest, I pleaded. You'll make me the happiest man ever." He picked her up and headed for the stairs.

"Where are we going?" she giggled..

"To have a prenuptial consummation of our marriage."

"Don't ever use that word with me, Ted," she hissed.
"Consummation?"
"No. Prenuptial."
"I'm not my father, Nora." He kissed her again and carried her to his room.

Ted nudged Nora awake the next morning. "Come on sleepyhead, let's get up."
"Must we?" she yawned.
He kissed her. "Yes, we must. Today we drive up to Okeechobee. It's a county seat and we can get married there quietly, and hopefully escape the tabloid wolves." He rolled out of bed. "I'm going to hit the shower. Go pack what you'll need for a few days. We'll get a marriage license today but we'll have to wait three days before we can marry."
Nora lowered her legs over the edge of the bed and stooped to gather the clothes she had stripped off the night before. She stood up. "Okay, I'll bathe in my room. Will we be coming back to Star Island?"
"Yes. We'll have to pack everything we want to take from here." He gave her a playful slap on her bare buttocks. "Let's get moving."
Nora went to her room and showered, and as she began to dress she spotted the straw hat Victor had given her for sightseeing in Nassau. She put it on and surveyed herself in the mirror. *It's been just three years but so much has happened in my life. I wonder what the next three will bring.*
As she finished packing, Ted came into the room. "Are you wearing that hat?" he asked.
"Yes. We'll drive my convertible with the top down. I want to keep the sun off my face." She paused. "Do you want to have breakfast before we leave? Then we won't have to stop along the

way. There's Danish and coffee in the kitchen. Cereal and fruit, too."

Ted grinned. "Suits me. I could use a little energy food after last night's workout."

They went downstairs. Nora started the coffeemaker, then sliced bananas into two bowls and covered them with cereal. "Here," she told Ted, "take these out to the patio. There's milk in the fridge. Get Danish from the cupboard. I'll bring the coffee as soon as it brews."

A few minutes later she joined him. She sat down and looked around. "You know, Ted, in some ways I'll miss this place though my life here has not been a very happy one."

He reached across the table and took her hands into his. "You're going to have a happy life on Samos. I promise you."

The roar of a lawn mower interrupted them. Nora smiled. "I guess the administrators are having the place spiffed up for the foreclosure sale. Do you have any idea of bidding on it?"

"Only if you really want to live here."

Nora shook her head. "Nope. Too many memories. I can be happy on Samos. Let's finish breakfast and hit the road to our future."

After they ate, Nora took the dishes into the kitchen. She carefully washed and dried them and put them away. *I don't want anyone who comes in here think we lived like pigs.*

As they drove up the Florida Turnpike ominous black clouds suddenly built up in front of them. Ted quickly pulled off the roadway and started raising the convertible top. Before it was completely closed, a torrential downpour struck.

"Phew!" Nora exclaimed. "If I hadn't had this hat on my head would have been soaked."

"Tell me about it," Ted laughed, wiping his face with a handkerchief. He reached up and locked the top latches.

Nora sobered. "Could this be a bad omen, Ted?"

DEATH TAKES A HONEYMOON

He put his arms around her. "I don't believe in omens but I do believe in playing it safe." The rain was coming down in buckets and the visibility almost nil. "We'll sit here until this storm blows over. These tropical cloudbursts don't last very long."

Other drivers also were being cautious, parking on the shoulder ahead and behind them.

When Nora and Ted reached Okeechobee they went straight to the courthouse and applied for a marriage license before checking into a motel.

"We have three days to kill, Nora. What would you like to do?"

Nora gave a little laugh. "I'd like to go to Disney World."

"You're joking!"

"I haven't been there since I was a kid. I'd really like to go."

"All right. Tomorrow we go to Disney World, but tonight we make love."

Nora tensed.

"Is anything wrong?" Ted asked anxiously.

"No. I just had a weird thought. Nothing really." *Victor had said "Tomorrow we go to Kushibasi. But we're on our honeymoon. Tonight we make love".*

DEATH TAKES A HONEYMOON

CHAPTER THIRTY

Nick Savage telephoned Jean. "I'm in Okeechobee. I followed Nora and Ted Patarkis up here. Get this. They got a marriage license. Now they're shacked up in a motel. My guess is they'll stay here for the three-day waiting period. Do you want me to tip the paparazzi?"
"No, not yet. Stay there and let me know the minute they get married."
"Okay. Hey, want to hear something weird? On the way up we ran into some heavy rain. They pulled off the road. I parked right behind them for about half an hour and they didn't have a clue they were being followed."

During the next three days Nora and Ted frolicked like college kids on Spring break. Nick phoned daily reports to Jean "They're giving me a wild chase. If I hear Small, Small World one more time I'm going to puke."
On the fourth day he called triumphantly "They did it, Jean! They just got married by a JP. I got pictures. Okay if I sell them to the tabloids?"
"Good work, Nick. Do whatever you want with the pictures. You can stop watching Nora now. Send me a final bill for your services."
"Does that mean I won't see you again?"
Jean's pulse quickened. "Oh, I think we can find some off-the-clock time together."
After hanging up, Jean sat in deep thought for a few minutes. From a desk drawer she took the earlier surveillance pictures Nick had given her and spread them on her desk. She touched a button on the intercom. "Roger, come to my office, please."

115

DEATH TAKES A HONEYMOON

"Is it important? I'm really busy."

Her voice rose. "It's very important. Come in here NOW!"

When Roger entered the office Jean pointed to her desktop. "Look at my new hobby. Collecting photographs."

Roger stared at the pictures and his heart sank. "So Nick Savage was following me."

She raised her eyebrows. "You know about Nick?"

"A security guard saw him hanging around Wayland Towers."

"He was mostly watching Nora. It's odd how often your paths crossed."

"Nothing happened at the condo," Roger blurted. "She was in a jam and I offered to help her for old times sake."

Jean frowned. "Sit down, Roger. You and I have to talk." She nervously drummed on the desk with her fingers as Roger drew up a chair. For a long moment she stared at him. "Marrying you was a big mistake, Roger. I didn't really want you. I just wanted to take you away from Nora."

His face reddened. "You just wanted to take me away from Nora? Why?"

"She was always so high and mighty. When I wanted the lead in school plays, she got it. When I wanted to be head cheerleader, she got it. I wanted to be the queen of the senior class but she got it. There was one thing she wanted that I could take from her. You."

"You could have saved yourself the trouble," he said bitterly, "she was going to dump me anyway."

"She dumped you after my father bought her off."

He shook his head. "You have a cruel streak in you, Jean."

Inwardly she smiled. *You don't know the half of it my dear husband.* "I want a divorce," she said calmly.

He looked at her in disbelief. "You want a divorce? How about my feelings? What about my position here at Wayland Construction?"

"You don't need the job. The stock my father gave you when

DEATH TAKES A HONEYMOON

we married, and the stock he left you in his will, makes you a millionaire. Of course, under the terms of the gifts I can buy the stock back at par value, which is far less than actual value. But I won't. I need you to help run the company."

She uncovered some papers. "I had my attorney draw up a simple no-fault divorce agreement. Everything is spelled out here. You'll sign a ten-year Personal Services contract giving you twice what you are now drawing, with annual cost-of-living adjustments, and you'll renounce all claims to any of my assets."

Roger read the document carefully. "I don't know. Maybe I should have a lawyer look at it."

"It's a take-it-or-leave-it offer!" Jean exploded. "I have enough evidence to divorce you on grounds of infidelity and you'll end up with nothing."

Roger shrugged. "I guess we'll both be better off."

Jean carefully folded the document until only the place for the signatures remained visible. She spoke into the intercom. "Wanda, please come in here and bring your notary seal."

Silence prevailed as they signed the paper and the Notary Public applied her seal. After the woman left, Jean gave a wan smile. "Let's try to be civilized about this. I think it best that you move out of the house right away. You don't have to take everything; just what clothes you'll need until the divorce is final. Now get back to work. We have a business to run."

Roger's heart soared as he left Jean's office. *I'll be free, and Nora's free. How lucky can a guy get?*

CHAPTER THIRTY-ONE

After the marriage ceremony Ted and Nora drove back to Miami. On the way to Star Island they stopped and picked up some cardboard cartons and sealing tape.

"You can pack the things you want to take from the house," Ted said. "I'll have a storage company pick them up and ship them to Samos when you're ready for them."

"There won't be much to pack. Just my clothes and a few keepsakes. I think I can get Erin to hold what I don't take to Samos."

On arriving home Ted called a travel agent. After talking for a few minutes he turned to Nora. "There's a noon flight to Athens tomorrow. Will you be ready to leave?"

"I'm ready now."

"All right, I'll make reservations."

"Fine. I'll call Erin after she gets home from work and see if she can take us to the airport. I'm going to let her have my car."

Later she called Erin. "Hey, sis, have I got news for you. Ted and I just got married."

"You didn't!"

"We did. We're leaving for Samos tomorrow. Can you store a few things for me until I'm ready for them?"

"Hey, let me catch my breath. Sure, there's plenty of room in the garage."

"Is there room there for a Mercedes convertible?"

"You're giving me your car?" Erin squealed.

"I may want to use it when I come to visit, but you can drive it whenever you want to. Can you take us to the airport tomorrow?"

"Sure. Gee, I can't believe it. I'll have a fancy set of wheels to chase Roger with."

"Come on, little sister, you're not going to try to break up

DEATH TAKES A HONEYMOON

Roger's marriage, are you?"

"I might not have to," Erin chortled. "Scuttlebutt around the office is that he and Jean are getting a divorce."

Nora remained silent for a moment. "I guess we both got surprises today. Well, I wish the best for him. Maybe you can be happy in a dinky little apartment together."

"You think it takes lots of money to be happy. I don't. I hope you'll be happy in your Greek villa with Ted. But don't sell Roger short. He practically runs the company since Mister Wayland died and I doubt that Jean will throw him out. Some day he might own the company."

"Dream on, little sister, dream on," Nora laughed. She hesitated. "Are Mother and Dad home?"

"No, they're off on an excursion with their bridge club. You know, Nora, you could have made more of an effort to reconcile with Dad after you married Victor."

"Don't preach to me, Erin," Nora snapped. *I should have made an effort to reconcile with my father? He's the stubborn one, practically disowning me because I went against his wishes.* "We'll come there in the morning and leave my car. It seats only two so you'll have to take us to the airport in yours. A cartage company will bring the things for you to store. Is that okay with you?"

"Sure, sis. Hey, I didn't mean to preach to you."

"And I didn't mean to snap at you. See you in the morning." She hung up.

"What was the big surprise?" Ted asked.

"Erin said there's a rumor that Roger Mangum is getting a divorce. She's had a crush on him for years."

"Will you see your parents before we leave?"

Nora pursed her lips. "No." She paused. "Erin will store my things and drive us to the airport."

"Good. I'll have your stuff picked up early in the morning." He

DEATH TAKES A HONEYMOON

made a telephone call. After he hung up he turned to Nora. "They'll be here by seven thirty. Let's get packing."

"Let me call George and Mimi first."

George answered her call."Hi, Nora, what's new?"

"Ted and I got married. We're leaving for Samos tomorrow."

"Wow, that's great. Wait a sec." He called to Mimi. "It's Nora, honey. She and Ted got married. Pick up the extension."

When Mimi came on the line Nora continued. "I want to thank you guys again for all you've done for me. When we get settled in Samos I want you to come visit, all expenses paid."

"Oh, I'd love that," Mimi exclaimed. "Does the offer include expenses for three?"

"You're pregnant!"

"Yeah. We just found out."

"Well, the offer is good for three, or four, or as many as arrive."

****

After signing the agreement with Jean, Roger returned to his office and worked feverishly to complete work that had been interrupted. He then drove home and packed necessary clothes into suitcases. Jean tactfully stayed away until he left for Wayland Towers.

Roger jumped out of bed the next morning, a song in his heart. *Now if I can only find where Nora is living.* His thoughts paused. *It's going to be awkward seeing Jean at the office, but this is what she wants.* He dressed quickly, left the condo and walked across the street to have breakfast. As he entered the restaurant, a headline on a tabloid newspaper caught his eye. WIDOW OF GREEK TYCOON WEDS HIS SON.

Oh, God, no. No!

A photo of Nora and Ted standing before a Justice of the Peace dominated the page.

Suddenly a chilling realization struck. *Jean knew!*

DEATH TAKES A HONEYMOON

DEATH TAKES A HONEYMOON

CHAPTER THIRTY-TWO

"It's just as beautiful as when I was here before," Nora thrilled as the plane flew low on the approach to the airport on Samos.

"What did you expect?" Ted laughed. "It's been less than three years. Things don't change that fast."

"Didn't the fire do a lot of damage?"

"To the forests, yes. But they recovered quickly. The towns and villages escaped any serious damage. The villa is pretty much the way you last saw it."

"Are Demetrious and Eleni still there?"

Ted's face sobered. "No, they left. They said they would not be comfortable since I was married to their daughter and you to my father. I didn't want to see them go but I can understand how they feel." He brightened. "Don't worry, there's plenty of good help available."

Ted's car was waiting when they landed. "I called ahead and told the storage garage people which flight we would arrive on, " he explained.

Deja vu, Nora thought as they drove through the village, past the luxury hotels, and onto the road running along the water. As they approached a sharp turn, she grasped Ted's arm. "This is where your mother was killed."

He braked to a quick stop. "Are you sure?"

"Yes. I remember the road turning away from the shore. Your father seemed to tense, and later he pointed it out from the terrace. Didn't he ever show you the place?"

"No. My father would never discuss the accident with me." He paused for a long moment "They were married for twenty-five years. Mother was very reserved and did not often show affection but I know he loved her. I also know he was having an affair with Sherry Lord. And there were other women."

"Do you think he was in any way responsible for her death?"

He shook his head slowly. "I don't want to believe that he had anything to do with it."

"That's what Sherry said."

He glanced at her sharply. "You discussed my mother's death with Sherry?"

"Yes. At the funeral chapel. She said she didn't want to believe that he had anything to do with the accident that killed your mother, or the one that put her husband in a coma."

. "I saw you go into the ante room with Sherry. When you came out I proposed to you the first time."

"You proposed?"

"You told me not to call you 'Mother' and I said I would rather call you my wife. Don't you remember?"

Nora smiled. "I remember."

Ted put the car back in gear and they drove on in silence. When they pulled into the courtyard of the villa, Nora pointed at the staircase leading upward. "Did you know I fell down those stairs, Ted?"

"Yes, Demetrious told me. What happened? Did you slip?"

"I really don't know. The forest was burning above here and we were hurrying to get away. As I started down I suddenly felt weak. The next thing I knew I was waking up in a hospital."

"You'll have to be careful on those steps." He laughed. "Do you want me to install an elevator?"

"Don't be silly." She got out of the car and headed for the stairway. "You bring the bags."

CHAPTER THIRTY-THREE

In the weeks following their arrival in Samos, the villa became a honeymoon retreat for Ted and Nora. He spent some time on the telephone and on his computer catching up on business affairs neglected during his absence, while she relaxed on the terrace. The nights were filled with wild, primeval passion.

A woman came in at regular intervals to houseclean. Nora prepared breakfasts and light lunches; they went out for dinners.

One afternoon he called to her from his den. "Would you like to go to Icaria tomorrow, honey?"

She yawned. "What's Icaria?"

He came out to where she reclined on a chaise lounge. "It's a nearby island that's considered to be among the most beautiful of the Greek islands. I have a business matter to take care of there."

She smiled up at him. "Business, business, business. You're just like your father."

"Oh, by the way," Ted added, "there's great shopping on Icaria."

Nora jumped up. "You said the magic word. Let's go."

"Hey," he laughed, "not until tomorrow. We'll take the hydrofoil from Samos Town in the morning and return home in the afternoon. My business there shouldn't take long. I'll hire a tour guide to show you around while I'm tied up"

"Will I need a guide to find the shops?"

"No. Many good shops are within walking distance of the docks. But there's a great old monastery you might want to see. If so, you'll have to dress appropriately. No bare head, arms or legs."

"Do I have to dress appropriately to enter the shops?"

Ted's eyes danced mischievously. "I think you could get into

most of them wearing nothing but your credit card."
"I'll wear shorts and a halter, thank you," Nora sniffed. She paused. "I'm ready to go anywhere as long as it's not Turkey."
Ted's jaw firmed. "We won't go to Turkey."

"Wow, this is really great," Nora thrilled as the hydrofoil skimmed the waves enroute to Icaria, "sure beats the ferry."
"Yes, much faster," Ted replied, "but you don't want to be on one if a storm hits. It can be a pretty rough ride."
"In a storm I don't want to be on anything that floats or flies."

When the boat docked they joined the stream of passengers going ashore.
"Whether you like it or not I'm hiring a guide for you," Ted said. He motioned to one of the men in a group holding signs. The man trotted over and Ted spoke to him in Greek. A broad grin lighted the guide's face.
"I told him to just follow you around and let you shop to your heart's content. He says he's married, too, and knows what makes a woman happy," Ted said. He glanced at his watch. "Try to be back here in about two hours. There are some great places where we can get lunch."
Nora tossed her shoulders. "When I'm shopping I lose all track of time."
"Well, the guide will see to it that you get back." He spoke a few words and the man nodded assent.

Urged by the guide, Nora returned to the docks at the proper time to find a jubilant Ted waiting. "I just sold a vineyard I owned here for a fabulous price. No matter how much you spent today I won't complain."

DEATH TAKES A HONEYMOON

"Well, that's one way you're not like your father. He blew his stack every time a credit card statement came in."

Ted pursed his lips. "Did it ever occur to you that he might have had good reasons to be concerned about your spending? During the last months of his life he had some staggering financial reverses. You and he lived far beyond your means."

"He never discussed finances with me," Nora replied lamely. She hesitated a moment. "I really don't know anything about your finances, Ted."

He put his arms around her shoulders. "I'll remedy that situation. I want you to know all about my business interests so that you can take over if anything happens to me. Come on, let's get something to eat and then catch the afternoon boat back."

He paid the guide, who bowed low and departed.

Ted and Nora left the boat when it docked at Samos Town, and as they headed for their car they unexpectedly ran into Demetrious. The former servant gave them a polite but cool greeting then began to shift uneasily as he conversed in Greek with Ted. After a few minutes he gave a quick bow and hurried away.

"He seemed kind of cold," Nora commented.

"Yes, he's having trouble accepting the divorce between his daughter and me. He says that Lydia has been at a retreat most of the time since we parted but is now living with him and Eleni. She's trying to kick her drug habit but it looks pretty hopeless." He paused and shook his head. "I really feel sorry for her."

Nora was silent as they headed for the car, but once seated she burst out "Do you still have feelings for her?"

Ted hesitated before answering. "Only pity. But I guess you really never forget your first love."

DEATH TAKES A HONEYMOON

No, Nora thought as Roger's face flashed through her head, *you never really forget your first love.*

The morning after their return from Icaria they were having breakfast on the terrace when the telephone inside the house rang. Ted went to answer it. Nora could hear him conversing with someone in Greek. His voice rose to a shout before he slammed down the receiver. He returned to the breakfast table, his face contorted in rage.
"Who was that? What happened?" Nora asked in alarm.
He sat down and buried his face in his hands. "This is impossible. This can't be."
"Will you please tell me what's going on?" Nora demanded.
Ted straightened up slowly. "That was my lawyer on the phone. Lydia has claimed that my divorce from her was obtained fraudulently as she was mentally and emotionally incompetent to make such a decision. A judge agreed with her and threw out the divorce decree. I'm still married to her."
"You're still married to her?" Nora screamed. "What about me?"
He stood up and began pacing back and forth. "Don't panic. We'll work it out. Some shyster lawyer must have convinced her that I'll get a big inheritance from my father's estate and that she should get a piece of it. She was plenty satisfied at the settlement I gave her when we divorced. I was real generous. Now I'll have to pay her off again." He sat back down.
"What about me?" Nora repeated. "What's going to happen to me?"
Ted reached across the table and took her hands in his. "I love you, Nora. I'll work things out with Lydia. But you'll have to get a quick divorce so I won't be charged with bigamy."
"Divorce?" Nora snorted, "If you were still married when we

married I could get an annulment."

"No, that would take too long and attract a lot of publicity."

"You want me to get a divorce here?"

"No, no, no. Samos authorities must not know we married." For a long moment he remained silent, then gave her a disarming smile. "Things got really tense between me and Lydia. She was on drugs much of the time. When I first thought about leaving her I did some research. You can get a divorce on the island of Guam after only a seven day's residence, and I won't have to be there."

Nora glared at him. "You want me to go to some backwater flyspeck island by myself? You're out of your mind. I love you, Ted, but this is asking too much."

"Guam is not a flyspeck island. It's an American territory and quite modern. You get a divorce there, and as soon as I work things out with Lydia come back here and we'll start all over."

Nora burst into tears and ran to the bedroom.

Later in the day Nora found Ted sitting at the computer in his den. She put her arms around him. "I know this mess is not your fault. I'm sorry I acted like a wimp."

He gave her a wan smile. "It was a shock for both of us but we'll work things out." He nodded toward the computer. "I've contacted an attorney in Guam, and made all the arrangements, and transferred funds electronically to cover the costs. I've made reservations for you to fly from here to Athens and from there to New York. You'll change planes in New York and again in Los Angeles for a direct flight to Guam. And I've made a reservation at a hotel there."

"You were sure I would go along with this, weren't you?" She shrugged. "I guess I have no choice. But could I go through Miami? Maybe I can get Erin to go to Guam with me."

DEATH TAKES A HONEYMOON

"Stay away from Miami until after the divorce. The tabloid jackals would eat you alive and spread the story all over the front pages. Perhaps Erin can join you on Guam. Want to call her?"

"No," Nora sighed, "I guess I'll be okay. When do I leave?"

"Tomorrow morning. My attorney is bringing the necessary papers you'll need from me. You'll pick up tickets at the airport for the flight to Guam and the return trip to Miami after you get the divorce." He put his arms around her. "I love you, Nora. We'll get through this nightmare. And we'll never be farther apart than a cellphone call."

DEATH TAKES A HONEYMOON

CHAPTER THIRTY-FOUR

As Nora exited the boarding gate at the Guam airport she abruptly stopped and stared in disbelief. "Jean, what are you doing here?"

Jean Mangum's mouth dropped open. "I might ask you the same thing, Nora."

"I'm here to get a divorce," Nora answered meekly.

A sardonic smile twisted Jean's face. "Welcome to the club. I just got my freedom and I'm outta here. What happened? Did your Greek prince turn into a toad?"

"There's nothing wrong with Ted," Nora retorted. "A little problem with his divorce from his first wife came up. As soon as he gets it straightened out I'm going back."

"Well, lotsa luck. I gotta run." As she headed for her plane Jean seethed inwardly. *If Nora thinks she'll get Roger now she had better think again. I'll see her in hell before I let that happen.*

Nora stood for a moment dumbfounded. *So Roger is free. How complicated can my life get?*

She picked up her luggage and took a cab to the hotel where Ted had made reservations. An islander took her bags from the cab, placed them on a dolly, and followed her to the hotel desk.

"You have a reservation for Nora Patarkis?" she asked the clerk.

The clerk glanced at his register. "Oh, yes, here it is. Welcome to Guam, Mrs. Patarkis. Will you be with us long?"

"No longer than I have to."

"Divorce?" the man smiled. "You'll find Guam a pleasant place to spend the waiting period. Beautiful weather, gorgeous scenery. Your room has a balcony overlooking the ocean. If you want to just relax, the hotel has a pool, spa and other amenities." He motioned to the bellhop. "Three fourteen."

DEATH TAKES A HONEYMOON

"Is this near?" Nora asked, showing the address of the lawyer Ted had contacted.

The clerk looked at it. "Oh, yes. It's just down the street. You can walk there from here."

"Thank you." She followed the bellhop to her room.

More than twenty-four hours had elapsed since she boarded the plane at Aristarhos Airport on Samos. Sleep had come in short episodes during the long flight. At first, while passing through time zones, she had tried to keep her watch adjusted, but finally gave up. Now she didn't have a remote clue as to the local time, only that it was still daylight and that she was completely exhausted. She undressed and, not bothering to shower, slid into bed. Sleep came instantly.

Nora woke up and glanced around the room. Sunlight streamed through a window opposite her bed. *Is it still the same day? Did I just have another in-flight nap?* She glanced at her watch. *No, a lot of hours have passed. I slept right through the night and I feel great!*

She showered and dressed and went down to the hotel's coffee shop.

"What do you people eat for breakfast here?" she asked a waiter.

A broad grin lighted the man's face. "Same things you eat Stateside, Missy. "Cereal, eggs, ham, sausage." He handed her a menu. "Nearly time for lunch but we still serve breakfast."

"Oh, what time is it?"

"Ten minutes after eleven."

Nora removed her watch from her wrist and set it. "Bring me coffee while I decide what to order. I r-e-a-l-l y need coffee."

When the waiter returned she was ready to order. "I'm pretty hungry. Bring me raisin bran with a chopped banana in it, a waffle with an egg on top, over light. Two sausage links. And leave the coffee pot."

After a leisurely breakfast Nora walked to the law office. A genial lawyer welcomed her. "Your husband made all the arrangements. You brought his power-of-attorney?"

"Yes." She handed it to him.

"Good. I'll get the proceedings started at once. In one week you will go before a magistrate, answer a few questions, and walk out a free woman."

"Being a free woman is not really what I want."

The lawyer's face sobered. "Yes, I was informed of your situation. Let's hope for what's best for all concerned."

Nora turned to leave. "Is it safe for me to walk along the beach?"

"Yes, quite safe. We don't have a high crime rate here."

As Nora strolled along she passed an elderly man looking seaward, apparently in deep thought. "Good afternoon," she greeted him cheerfully.

The man snapped out of his reverie and looked around. "Oh, good afternoon, Nora."

Nora's eyes opened wide. "How did you know my name?"

"I was in the hotel lobby when you checked in and overheard your conversation with the clerk. It's not every day I see a pretty Irish girl with a Greek last name getting a divorce." He stuck out his hand. "My name is Leonardo. I'm Italian."

Nora took his hand, laughing. "I guessed that. I mean, that you're Italian. You know why I'm here but what brings you to Guam?"

"Memories, Nora, memories. Good memories. Bad memories." He pointed to the beach. "This is where they came ashore."

DEATH TAKES A HONEYMOON

"They?"

"The Japanese. We put up a helluva fight but they overwhelmed us."

"You were in the war? My grandfather was in the war but he would never talk about it."

Leonardo shook his head. "A lot of old soldiers don't like to talk about their war experiences. Afraid people will think they're bragging and exaggerating the part they played. And there are some who just don't want to bring back bad memories."

"You have bad memories of Guam?" Nora asked.

"Yes. I was taken prisoner and spent nearly four years in a work gang right here on Guam. Those are bad memories."

"You were not treated well?"

"No, we were not treated well. When our boys came back to retake the island the Jap guards were going to kill all the prisoners. One of their officers stopped them. He was the only one half-way decent to us the whole time. I kinda wish he had survived."

"He was killed?"

"They were all killed. Japanese soldiers never surrendered." He turned and gazed out to sea. "Memories are insidious, Nora. No matter how hard you try to get rid of them they just won't go away."

Memories, Nora thought. *Some good memories with Victor but too many bad ones. Mostly good memories with Ted. And with Roger?* She closed her eyes tightly as if to shut out the vivid images of herself in Roger's arms.

Leonardo suddenly brightened. "Will you have dinner with me? And perhaps a dance after?"

Nora hesitated. *Dinner and a dance. That's how it started with Victor.* She shook her head. "I'm not really in a socializing mood right now. Thanks anyway." She turned and hurried away.

DEATH TAKES A HONEYMOON

The waiting period passed leisurely for Nora. She relaxed at the hotel pool or played cards with other women here to get divorces. "Guam is not much of a shoppers' paradise," one of the women had sniffed.

Leonardo was still a guest at the hotel and they exchanged pleasantries when passing. One morning while she was eating breakfast he came into the dining room and she motioned for him to join her.

The final divorce hearing went much as the attorney had told her it would. A magistrate asked a few questions. Children issue of this marriage? None. Division of community property? Waived.

Nora had hesitated when Ted's lawyer asked her to sign the waiver, but she quickly realized that except for a few personal belongings everything was Ted's before they married. For a marriage of such short duration she would find it hard to establish a claim to any of his assets.

The proceedings in the Guam courtroom ended quickly. The magistrate, the attorney and Nora shook hands all around, and Nora walked out single again.

She lost no time confirming her flight from Guam to Miami. On the morning after the divorce decree was handed down she took a taxi to the airport. When she reached the departure gate she saw Leonardo waiting to board the same plane she would take.

"Good morning, Nora," he smiled. "Where are you headed?"

"Miami."

He shook his head. "Too bad it's not New York. We might still have had that dinner and dance together."

The boarding call sounded and Nora took her seat in First Class. Later, as the plane filled from the rear forward, Leonardo passed her, heading for a seat deeper in the plane. They never met again.

DEATH TAKES A HONEYMOON

CHAPTER THIRTY-FIVE

Weary from the long flight, Nora trudged down the concourse at Miami International Airport. To her surprise, as she exited the security gate, she saw Roger.

"What are you doing here, Roger," she exclaimed. "Erin was supposed to meet me."

Roger grinned. "Erin came down with some kind of bug and asked George to meet you. But he and Mimi were scheduled to go on duty so George asked me to meet you." He gave her a quick hug. "The condo is still available, Nora."

****

In the days following Nora's return to Miami, Ted called frequently, optimistic at first but less so as time passed. Lydia had moved back to the villa. "But I'm not sleeping with her," Ted added quickly. Then one night as Nora was getting ready to crawl into bed the phone on her bedside stand rang. It was Ted., his voice taut with anguish..

"Lydia went off the deep end and attacked me with a kitchen knife."

"Are you hurt?" Nora asked in alarm.

"No. A few minor cuts, that's all. I was able to disarm her. She's been committed to a mental hospital, and the doctors say she might be there for a long time. I won't be able to divorce her while she's there." He paused. "I want you to come back to Samos, Nora. There's no reason we can't have a good life together."

Nora didn't answer.

"Are you there, Nora? Did you hear what I said?"

"I heard you." Seconds ticked by before she spoke again. "I love you, Ted, but I will not be to you what Sherry Lord was to your father. I wish things had turned out differently for us. I really do. This

DEATH TAKES A HONEYMOON

is goodbye, Ted. I'm sorry."

She clicked off the phone and gave Roger a wan smile. "So ends another sordid chapter in my life."

Roger took her in his arms. "There'll be no more sordid chapters in your life, Nora. You and I were meant to be together and we will be until death do us part."

Nora shuddered. "That sounds so ominous."

He kissed her tenderly. "Let's get married right away, before anything else comes between us."

She snuggled against him. "All right, but there's something I have to do first. I have to make peace with my father."

"Do you want me to go with you?"

"No, I'd rather go alone."

"All right. Tomorrow morning while you go see your father I'll start making arrangements for the wedding."

Nora stood in trepidation before the entrance to the O'Neal family home. *Damn, I lived in this house most of my life and now I'm afraid to walk in.* She tapped lightly on the door and her father opened it. He gave her a scathing glare.

"So me sinful daughter returns."

"May I come in, Daddy?"

He stepped aside and she entered. "Roger and I are getting married and we want your blessing."

He opened his mouth wide in mock surprise. "So, it's me blessin' ye be wantin' now is it? Ye who turned away from the mother church. Ye'll get no blessin' from me."

"Give her your blessing, Terrence," Nora's mother demanded sharply.

"You stay out of this, Maureen."

"I will not stay out of it! You've been a stubborn old goat,

DEATH TAKES A HONEYMOON

Terrence O'Neal. I wanted Nora to marry in our church as much as you did." She crossed herself. "May Heaven forgive her that she didn't. You will not turn your back on our firstborn, Terrence O'Neal." Her voice broke. "You will not turn your back on our firstborn."

Terrence's eyes narrowed. "Ye will be marryin' in our church this time, Nora?"

"I'd like to, Daddy, really I would, but I don't think it's possible. I've been married twice outside the church and I've been divorced. Roger's been divorced."

Her father shook his head doggedly. "In the eyes of the church ye've never bin married. There be ways. Arrangements kin be made."

"It would take too long. Roger and I want to get married now."

"Give her your blessing," Maureen O'Neal sobbed.

Nora's father walked over slowly and put his arms around her. He pressed her head against his shoulder. "Ye've bin a big disappointment to me, Nora."

Erin O'Neal, who had been sitting silently across the room, suddenly exploded. "Don't expect me to be your Maid of Honor this time. You know how much I love Roger. You dumped him to marry Victor, and just when I have a chance with him you come back. Now I guess I'll have to wait until you're dead."

Nora pulled away from her father's grasp. "What a terrible thing for you to say, Erin. You don't mean that."

Erin's eyes flashed. "I guess you'll take the car from me too. I hate you, Nora. I hate you." She ran from the room, tears flowing.

Nora started to follow but her mother stopped her. "Let her cry it out. She's young, she'll get over it."

****

"This is deja vu all over again," George Evans quipped as he and

DEATH TAKES A HONEYMOON

Roger stood in the anteroom of the same church where Roger and Jean had married., "but this time you're marrying the right girl."

Roger shook George's hand. "You're the best friend a guy ever had, George, and Nora told me how good you and Mimi have been to her. I'm glad Mimi felt up to being Matron of Honor after Erin took sick."

"What's wrong with Erin?"

"She caught a bug of some kind. I hope it's nothing serious. Erin's a great kid. I like her. If Nora hadn't come back into my life I might even had made a play for Erin."

George grinned. "You couldn't have kept her away from you with a baseball bat." His eyes twinkled. "Did you invite Jean to the wedding?"

"Ha! No way. She and Nora are not the best of friends. Anyhow, she's with her new boyfriend, the PI she had watching Nora and me. They're on an inspection cruise aboard the Caribbean Lady. She inherited a major share of the ship from her father and now she's considering bidding on Victor Patarkis' interest when the courts put it up for auction."

George's face sobered. "Didn't your father want to be your Best Man?"

Roger snorted. "He couldn't stay off the booze long enough. I can't figure what's gotten into him. The whole time we were on the job in Turkey he never had more than a beer or two. Since we got back he's hardly had a sober day. On the happy side, Nora and her father made up and he's giving her away."

"Where are you and Nora going on your honeymoon?" George asked.

"Things are too hectic at the office for me to get away right now. We're going to spend a few days at the Seabreeze Hotel at the beach. We're moving into the penthouse at Wayland Towers but it's not quite finished. To complicate things, the buyer of the unit where we've been living wants to take possession."

George raised his eyebrows. "The Seabreeze? That's a coincidence. Our precinct captain is retiring and we're holding a bash for him there tomorrow night."

The first strains of the wedding march drifted into the room. George put his arm around Roger's shoulder. "Come on, pal. Like I said once before, you don't want to keep your bride waiting."

DEATH TAKES A HONEYMOON

CHAPTER THIRTY-SIX

Roger and Nora returned to their room after a late swim in the hotel pool. As they entered, Roger's cellphone rang. He answered, and his temper rose as he listened. "Dammit, Jose, can't you take care of it?" There was a pause as the caller spoke. "All right," Roger fumed, "I'll get there as soon as I can."

He turned to Nora. "My dad got into a drunken brawl in a bar near here and busted up some fixtures. The manager is threatening to call the cops if the damage isn't paid for. I've got to go get him out of there."

"Do you have to?" Nora pouted, "We're on our honeymoon."

Roger gave her a quick kiss. "I won't be gone long. Order some champagne and we'll celebrate big time when I get back." He dressed hurriedly and left.

Some honeymoon, Nora thought. She called Room Service. "Send a bottle of Dom Perignon to seven twenty-four."

"Yes, ma'am, but there will be a delay of fifteen to twenty minutes. The waiters are quite busy."

"All right. Tell the waiter if there's no answer when he knocks to come on in and leave the champagne. I might be in the bathroom."

After she hung up, Nora stripped off her bathing suit and surveyed herself in a full-length mirror. *Hmm, I'm not showing yet. I wonder if I should tell Roger now that I'm carrying Ted's baby? I'll have to tell him soon.* She shrugged and started for the bathroom.

Suddenly she clutched her breast. *Oh, no. Not now. Not here.* She stumbled to the bed and lay down.

She did not hear the waiter's knock or see him enter the room

****

DEATH TAKES A HONEYMOON

Nora's body had been removed, and the forensic team was finishing an examination of the room when Roger burst in. He spotted George and the other policemen. "George, what are you doing here? Where's Nora?"

"Where the hell have you been?" George demanded.

Roger's gaze darted wildly around the room. "Where's Nora? Has something happened to Nora?"

"She's dead, Roger."

"Oh, God, no." Roger collapsed into a chair and buried his face in his hands. "What happened?"

Sgt. Webb walked over to them. "Is this the woman's husband?"

"Yes, Roger Mangum," George answered.

The sergeant gave Roger a steely stare. "Where have you been, Mister Mangum?"

"I went to get my father out of a jam." He sobbed. "What happened to Nora?"

"We won't know until we get the coroner's report. Meanwhile, I suggest that you not leave town."

Roger glanced up sharply. "You don't think I had anything to do with her death, do you?" He looked imploringly at George. "Oh, God! You know I'd never do anything to hurt Nora."

George patted him on the back. "I know that, Roger." He turned to Sgt Webb. "Okay if I take him out of here, Phil?"

"Sure, go ahead."

George took Roger's arm. "Come on, you're going home with me."

DEATH TAKES A HONEYMOON

****

Erin, George and Roger gazed solmnly at Nora's still form in the casket. Mimi tenderly comforted Terrence and Maureen O'Neal a short distance away.

"She was told when she failed the high school cheerleader physical that she had a heart condition," Erin murmured. "But she didn't want anyone to know there was anything less than perfect about her. The coroner's report revealed that her heart finally gave out."

"We all loved her." George's voice was hoarse. "It would not have made any difference."

Roger suppressed a sob. "Yes, we all loved her and we'll never forget her, but life goes on."

Erin touched his arm lightly. "Yes, life goes on."

THE AGENT/MANAGER

One foot planted on the chest of his fallen foe, the young warrior stood dazed and awed at the attention being given him. Hastily scrawled in charcoal on the sweatband across his forehead was the word "Abrams".

A horde of scribes pressed close, roughly jostling each other in an attempt to gain a better position, their voices rising in a loud cacophony as each tried to make himself heard. Eventually one voice boomed above the others. "What means the word on your sweatband?"

The young man squirmed uneasily.

"Tell them, David," a bearded man at his elbow urged. "Tell them."

The crowd fell silent to hear the victor's words.

"Well, you know, it's like I used an Abrams sling to, you know, kill Goliath."

"And," the bearded man added quickly, "it was an Abrams pellet, carefully honed in our own quarries for the precise shape and weight to assure the greatest accuracy, that felled the mighty giant."

"How came you to be chosen to face Goliath?" one of the scribes shouted.

David hesitated nervously. "Well, you know, it's like, somebody had to, you know, get the job done. I was, you know, just in the right place at the right time."

Again a bedlam of sound arose as the scribes shouted more questions. A hawk-faced man edged up to David.

"Say no more, David. The story tellers will pay many pieces of silver for the story of your life. I am Nathan, son of Jacob. I know of these things. Clasp my right arm with yours as a sign that I shall speak

THE AGENT/MANAGER

for you on those matters."

To a young shepherd boy who had never owned even one piece of silver, the vision of a handful of shiny cins was overwhelming. A look of bewilderment crossed his face as he locked arms with the stranger. Nathan immediately took charge.

"All right, you men, back off. My boy has had a hard fight and he's tired. He'll speak to you later. Now make way. Make way." He placed an arm around David's shoulder and led him from the field of battle. "You're a hero, David, and I'm going to make you a very rich man."

The spoils of victory were not long in coming. Nathan appeared the next morning bubbling with enthusiasm. "Reboth, the butcher, will give two fatted calves — one for me and one for you — for saying you built strength for the battle by eating meat from his cattle."

David frowned. "But the only meat I have ever eaten is the flesh of my father's sheep."

Nathan shrugged his annoyance. "That is of small consequence. Trust me, David, I know that which I do. Take the calf."

Twinges of conscience bothered David, but as offers continued to pour in — great loaves of bread from the baker, casks of wine from the vintner — he brushed guilt feelings aside. After all, he rationalized, I am a hero, and these are deserved rewards for a hero. The naive shepherd boy was rapidly becoming sophisticated.

But Nathan was taking half of everything. By what right? David thought angrily. He called Nathan to him. "From this day on you shall take but one part in ten of my bounty."

Nathan protested vehemently. "But we have a pact. We clasped arms on it."

"True," David replied coldly, "but was there ever any mention of what your share would be? You will accept what I give you. Now go."

THE AGENT/MANAGER

As time passed David's wealth grew and he became renowned for his skill and valor in battle. Summoned to the royal court by King Saul, he was given the hand of Saul's daughter, Michal, in marriage. But his relationship with Nathan deteriorated steadily. After Nathan involved him in a particularly odorous transaction, David dismissed his confident.

Nathan was furious. "You'll rue this day, David. I made you and I can break you." He stormed from the room.

Losing no time, Nathan went to King Saul. "Sire, was not David in your service at the time he slew Goliath?"

Saul nodded acknowledgment.

"Then, Sire," Nathan smiled triumphantly, "the treasures heaped on him as a result of his victory belong to you. David has stolen from you!

The king eyed him with contempt. "Did you not take part of the spoils?"

Nathan prostrated himself on the ground. "Sire, I was but a lowly servant doing the bidding of my master."

With a wave of his hand, Saul dismissed the groveling man.

Saul now faced a serious dilemma. By his own law, the penalty for stealing from the royal court was death. But David was much beloved by the people, so taking his life was unthinkable. With heavy heart, Saul called David to his quarters.

"My son, Nathan has spread word among the people that you have stolen from me. I can deny this, but there will always be doubt in the minds of some. Powerful men conspire to take my throne from me. If I am to remain king, I must enforce my own laws. I love you too dearly to have your head. However, I must punish you." He heaved a deep sigh. "From this moment you are banished from my court and must leave Israel." He paused. "As further penance, you must take Nathan with you."

THE AGENT/MANAGER

A despondent David rode out of Israel with a small band of followers. But Nathan's eyes blazed with excitement. "David, the landowners of Judea will welcome you as a protector and you can exact much tribute from them. I know of these things. Clasp my arm as a sign of friendship and I will make you King of Judea." He paused, studying David's face intently. "And who knows? Some day you may lead an army back into Israel and seize the throne of Saul."

The chronicles reveal that David WAS exiled by Saul, DID become King of Judea, and after Saul and his sons fell in a battle with the Philistines, DID return to Israel and become king. Nathan's part in these events cannot be corroborated.

A WALK IN THE PAST

Paris in the Spring. Birds warbling in the treetops. Impudent squirrels contesting pigeons for tidbits tossed by park-goers. A profusion of flowers gifting the light breeze with the elusive fragrance of a rare French perfume. All nature seemed in harmony as I began my daily walk in the park until I saw, sitting on a bench, a ghost from my past.

"Linda? Linda Sims?" My question was tentative.
The woman looked up, studied me a moment, then jumped up screaming. "Clive Kendall? Oh my God, is it really you? I can't believe it! It must be thirty years since we were together." She wrapped her arms around me.

"A little longer than that," I replied. I returned her hug and stepped back. "Let me look at you. You're just as beautiful as you were then."

She sniffed. "It takes eons of time in beauty parlors, and tons of money spent on cosmetics and spas to become beautiful. Back then I was just very pretty. But we were young and we were in love."

"Well, whatever it took, it worked," I replied, "you really look great. You're the last person I ever expected to see in Paris. What are you doing here?"

"I live on the Riviera. I came up to take care of a business matter. What brings you here?"

"Nostalgia, I guess. I'm revisiting places I visited over the years. Kind of a trip down memory lane."

She lowered her gaze. "Was I in any of those memories?"

"You bet you were! Almost all of them." I hugged her again. "You know, you broke my heart when you left without so much as a

A WALK IN THE PAST

goodbye kiss. I looked everywhere but couldn't find you."

"I didn't want you to find me. If I saw you again, then, all of my carefully made plans for the future would have gone down the sewer."

I grabbed her hand. "Come on. I'm going for a walk in the park. Walk with me and we can catch up on what's happened since — since we last saw each other."

"I'd like that."

We strolled along, carefully exchanging banalities, as if each feared initiating a meaningful dialogue. At an embarrassing lull in the conversation Linda blurted out "We were in this park before, Clive."

"Yes, this and a lot of other parks."

Ahead four nude marble nymphs playfully splashed each other in a sparkling fountain pool. Linda ran over, sat on the basin rim, and dangled one hand in the water. As I sat down beside her she smiled. "Remember 'our' fountain in Red Square in Rome?"

"Oh, yes, good old Red Square. That wasn't its real name but because of all the posters plastered on the walls by the Italian Communist Party, that's the name we gave it. I'll never forget the time we went skinny-dipping in the fountain after midnight and hid, buck-naked, behind a hedge when a police patrol drove by."

Linda giggled. "If they had seen us we would have had to change the name to Red Face Square."

"The most traumatic memory I have of our time together in Rome is of when pickpockets got all of our money and we fished coins out of Trevi Fountain to buy a meal at that Greek cafeteria on the Via Quarto Fontana. That was one of the few times in my life I was really scared."

"I was pretty scared, too. If we had been caught we might still be in an Italian jail."

"That's not what concerned me. They might have given us a slap on the wrist, that's all. What made my insides churn was being broke in a foreign land with you depending on me to get us out of the

A WALK IN THE PAST

mess. We were fortunate that my parents cabled us some money." She tossed her head. "My stomach churned because I was hungry."

I gave her a wistful look. "I liked that cafeteria. The food was plain but the portions large and the prices small. I was in Rome recently. The cafeteria is still there but the posters are gone from Red Square. Incidently, I repaid the Trevi with a handful of coins."

Linda seemed more at ease now, the emotional shock from our unexpected reunion slowly subsiding. "We did have a ball, didn't we? One thing I learned in Venice is not to horse around in a gondola. I can still hear that gondolier screaming at us when we nearly capsized his boat. I can't imagine what would have happened if we had fallen into that polluted water. We might be lying in an Italian cemetery now."

She smiled. "Remember how the young backpackers gathered at the railroad station in Vienna? Some of the kids actually made out under blankets on the hard tile floor."

"Yes, I remember. You and I were somewhat more discrete. We usually found a little *pension* in which to spend the nights."

Linda sighed. "Backpacking around Europe was such a lark in those days."

"They still do it, Linda."

"Backpack?"

"The kids still congregate at the railroad station. What they do under their blankets I don't know."

She gave me a playful punch on the arm. "Don't tell me! You were in Vienna recently." She turned serious. "We were so good together. Sometimes I wonder why we parted."

"Oh, it was simple enough. I wanted a safe, secure job in the city and a nice little home in the suburbs. You wanted a castle in Spain or anywhere else as long as it was pretentious." I paused. "Did you

A WALK IN THE PAST

find your dream castle?"

"Yes. Three times. But the lords of the castles were such dull, stuffy men. In the end, though, I think they were as glad to end the marriages as I was. Their parting gifts were most generous." She looked into my eyes. "How about you? Did you get what you wanted?"

I nodded. "I liked my job on Wall Street, and I married a lovely girl whose greatest joy was puttering around the garden of our home in the suburbs. And later supervising the gardeners on our estate at the lake. She had only one serious vice — fast driving. She died in a car accident two years ago."

Linda murmured a few words of sympathy then slipped into a pensive mood, looking down and slowly stirring the water with one finger. "I guess we were pretty crazy when we were young and we made mistakes we later regretted, but as the old song goes..." she sang the words softly, "...we did have fun, and no harm done."

Abruptly she stood up and started down the path. I quickly joined her.

From off to one side a voice called. "So, handsome American gentleman, you do have a lady."

I looked in the direction of the sound. As she had every day since my arrival in Paris a girl sat there perched on a high stool before an easel holding a partially finished painting, a pallet in one hand, a brush in the other. Examples of her art, mostly nude or near-nude reclining female figures reminiscent of Goya's *Naked Maja* rested on the grass behind her.

Raven hair, framing a pixie face, streamed down the girl's bare back to form small circlets at the belt line of her white short shorts. Long tapered legs, crossed at the ankles, ended in tiny sandal-clad feet. A flowered halter restrained petite, perfectly molded breasts.

But the things about her that captivated me most were her eyes, the largest, deepest, most lustrous emerald-green eyes I have ever

A WALK IN THE PAST

seen. On other days, when she had a group of spectators watching her paint, I edged close and surreptitiously studied those eyes.

I guided Linda over to the girl. "How did you know I'm an American?"

The artist shrugged. "I inquired around. Every day you come by here, always alone. I ask myself 'why does such a handsome gentleman not have a lady?'. But I see that you do have a lady, a most splendid lady who would make such a magnificent painting. I could sketch that beautiful face right here but..." she gestured toward her display "...I do my best work in the boudoir." She gave me a pointed look. "I am very good at what I do in the boudoir."

Linda tugged at my elbow. Come on. She's flattering us in the hope of making a sale. Anyway, I have to go get ready for a meeting with my bankers."

When we reached Linda's hotel she opened the door to her room and flashed me a coquettish smile. "Coming in? I can postpone my meeting."

I shook my head. "No. Too many years have passed. I might only embarrass myself. Let's always remember it the way it was."

Her face darkened, and in a flash I recalled what a vixen she could be when things didn't go as she wanted them to.

Just as quickly her features softened. She gave me a light kiss. "Well, if you change your mind you know where I'm staying."

For a long moment I stared at the closed door after she entered the room. Then I turned and hurried down the hall.

Green eyes might still be in the park.

THE FUGITIVE

For Judd, running was a way of life. Running from one menial job to another. In town after town. Running from untenable social situations. But mostly running from himself.

A shy, inhibited man, Judd didn't make friends easily. With either men or women. Especially women. Women had always meant bad news for him. Except for Marsha. Marsha seemed to understand him from the start.

This dreary wintery night Judd slouched in the hard plastic bucket seat of a bus station, his slight frame wrapped in a too-large overcoat. A stocking cap, pulled low over his ears and to the tops of steel-rimmed glasses, covered his thinning hair. Waiting for another bus. To another town. To another job.

Emporia had not been kind to Judd and he was glad to be leaving. Except for Marsha. He would miss Marsha. She was different from other women he had met. Marsha was nothing like that tramp, Lila, who worked beside him on the loading dock back in Plainsville. That was before Emporia. Before Buntstown. Before Headley.

Lila bragged she'd had every man in the warehouse. Judd cringed at the memory of the time she lured him to a far corner behind a pile of crates and barrels. Things didn't go at all well. Afterward she told everybody he had tried to but couldn't, and they all roared with laughter. Humiliated, Judd ran. Ran.

When a policeman entered the bus station waiting room, pausing inside the door to rub his hands together briskly and to stomp snow and slush from his boots, Judd slumped lower in his seat and partially covered his face with a newspaper.

THE FUGITIVE

    He had always wondered why he felt uncomfortable around policemen. Perhaps it went back to the boyhood incident when he was stopped outside a five and dime and accused of stealing a yoyo. He realized now that his accuser then was a security guard, not a policeman. But the man did wear a uniform, and since then men in blue uniforms made Judd feel uneasy.
    Back then Judd finally convinced the store manager that the yoyo he was playing with was of a brand the store didn't carry. But it was a close call. Dared by his schoolmates to do it, he had toyed with the idea of pocketing a glittering, rhinestone-embedded whistling yoyo from the store's stock.
    After the confrontation with the security man, dreading to face the taunts of his peers, Judd slipped out of the store and ran home.

    The policeman who entered the bus station glanced idly around the room, went to the potbelly stove to warm himself for a few minutes, then left to continue his rounds.

    Near midnight a bus rolled in, crunching through the crust of freezing slush on the driveway. Judd was glad to see that there were few passengers aboard as he made his way down the aisle and dropped into a seat near the rear of he bus. He prayed no one would take the seat beside him. He didn't feel like talking to strangers tonight.
    Absent-mindedly he watched the snow swirling against the window as the bus pulled away from the station — jolting a little as it crossed frozen ruts — and threaded its way into highway traffic.
    As the bus headed down the road, Judd's thoughts drifted to another snowy night like this, and anther bus ride, when he was a small boy. If his mother had really loved him why did she send him off to live with a distant relative, a woman who really didn't want him

THE FUGITIVE

either? But that was the story of his life, Judd thought with a sigh. Women always rejected him. Gradually he dozed off.

A rest stop call roused him from a fitful sleep, but he remained in his seat as the other passengers slowly filed out. Not until all had disappeared inside the small bus station and he could see no one standing on the wooden sidewalk did he leave the bus and enter the small restaurant.

He sat at the counter, and a smiling waitress placed a steaming cup of coffee before him. She made a few flip comments on the weather then went on to her next customer.

Marsha was like that. That's how they met, he and Marsha. At the factory lunchroom in Emporia. She served him coffee, spoke a few cheerful words, and moved on. But she kept coming back to him between customers. Guardedly he studied her movements and listened, entranced, to her laughter. His coffee grew cold, and then the factory whistle signaled the end of the lunch period and he had to hurry back to his machine.

From the corners of his eyes Judd watched the friendly waitress at the bus stop. His coffee grew cold and then the bus horn sounded, calling the passengers back aboard.

In the darkened coach Judd's thoughts wove erotic fantasies about the pert waitress he had just left behind. And he thought about Marsha, too.

After that first meeting at the lunch counter he had eagerly anticipated his midday visits with her. And she seemed to enjoy talking with him. She told him little things about herself, and he timidly revealed some details about his life. Not too much. But she seemed interested.

THE FUGITIVE

Several weeks passed before she surprised him with an invitation to dinner at her house.

Throughout the meal Judd fidgeted nervously with his food, eating hardly anything. Not that the food wasn't good; Marsha was an excellent cook.

After the table was cleared, as they stood in the kitchen, he clumsily put his arms around her, fumbling with the fastenings of her dress, and pressing his lips against hers. Startled, she pushed him away.

He stepped back, confused. She *had* invited him over, hadn't she? At night. This is what she wanted, wasn't it? Then Judd saw a look in Marsha's eyes he had never seen before. A look of scorn? A look of contempt? No! Suddenly he realized it was a look of pity. She didn't really like him, she pitied him!

Nervous tension building up all evening suddenly exploded. He lashed out, striking her face. Caught off balance by the unexpected blow she fell, striking her head on the edge of a granite countertop.

When the bus groaned to a stop and the passengers began gathering their belongings — the shopping bags, the string-tied boxes — Judd knew this was the end of the run and he had to get off. Off into another hostile town. Off to another un-fulfilling job...

Then he saw them. Two policemen talking with the bus driver, and the driver pointing toward the rear of the bus.

Judd cowered against the seat in the desperation of a cornered animal. An anguished scream escaped his lips. "Oh, God! Oh, God! She didn't have to die. She - - didn't - - have - - to - - die!"

THE CAD

"Hey, I didn't mean for you to walk in on me and Ellen. You shouldn't have come home early without letting me know you were coming."

"So it's my fault I caught you cheating? Oh, Gary, what is it about me that made you want another woman?"

He squirmed. "Don't get me wrong, baby. Living here with you has been great. It's just that Ellen is so... so exciting."

"Well, get your things together and get out. We're through."

"So that's the way it is? After all we've been to each other it's 'get your things together and get out', just like that?" He paused. "We can still be friends, can't we?"

She didn't answer.

He cupped her chin in one hand and gazed pleadingly into her eyes. "Friends?"

Tears trickled down her cheeks and her lips quivered. "All -- all right. Friends."

A broad smile lighted his face. He put his arms around her. "There's nothing wrong with two friends going to bed together and sharing a few goodbye kisses, is there?"

She jerked away, her eyes flashing, and delivered a sharp slap to the side of his face.

"You bastard! I would rather go to bed with a rattlesnake than go to bed with you again."

"Cut!" the director shouted "That's a wrap for today, people. Tomorrow we shoot the nightclub scene so everybody here by eight sharp. And know your lines. We'll have a lot of extras on the set and we're on a tight budget. Let's get it right the first time."

Brad gingerly touched the side of his face with a fingertip. "You really take your role character seriously, don't you Laurie? That hurt."

She laughed. "I really didn't intend to hit you that hard. Your

THE CAD

'Gary' character is such a philandering pig I guess I momentarily lost control of myself."

He gave her a wide grin. "I'll forgive you if you'll go to dinner with me. Then maybe later..."

She gave him a playful shove. "You take your role character seriously, too, don't you? I'll go to dinner with you, period.

MY LIFE WILL NEVER BE THE SAME

What made me leave Interstate 10 and strike out over the Arizona desert in my new sports utility vehicle I can't imagine. Did some capricious God of Fate control my hands on the steering wheel, or was it my own personal guiding angel?

SUVs are built for adventure, I know, and perhaps the wild exhilaration at owning a new toy, coupled with a need to clear my head so as to make a rational decision in solving the dilemma sitting beside me, led to my rash move.

Anyway, because of my impulsiveness that fateful day just 274 days ago (I counted every one of them), my life will never be the same again. But let's go back to the beginning.

The day started as any bright, cheerful, happy day starts. Then Tina called. Tina always called when she had problems or needed money; the two events usually coincided. To Tina, a divorce decree was just a scrap of paper.

Divorce had been her idea. "There's no other man in my life, Blake," she insisted, "and I have no intention of there ever being one. I just got married too young and never had a chance to probe the depths of my psyche, to find the 'real me'. I went from my parents' house to your house, with no period of transition. I need to experience more of life."

I really love this little bubblehead, and I pleaded for her to reconsider, promising her as much space as she wanted. But she remained adamant.

When we parted I gave her a generous cash settlement, but she let it slip away. There was the investment in that 'darling little florist shop', when she knew nothing about flowers. And then the 'chic little French bakery': during our marriage not so much as a bran muffin came out of her oven.

"Blake," her voice on the phone was breathless, "I need to borrow twenty-five thousand dollars. Just for a few weeks. It's a chance to make millions."

"Twenty-five grand? Have you flipped your wig?"

"Oh, that's not a lot of money to invest when the potential profits are so great."

I sighed. "What is it this time?"

"It's too hush-hush to talk about on the phone. Come on over. And bring your checkbook."

"Okay, I'll come over. But don't count on me to back another hare-brained scheme. Tell you what, I was just getting ready to take my new SUV out for a test drive. Go along with me and we can discuss what's on your mind as we ride."

As I drove to Tina's place I pondered my dilemma. I wanted her back but I didn't want to buy her back. If I refuse to give her the money will that end any chance of a reconciliation? She can be very bullheaded. Not that I couldn't afford the money; a modest investment in an upstart computer software company has brought returns beyond my wildest expectations.

Tina was waiting at the curb when I pulled up. She jumped in, babbling excitedly. "Silver, Blake, tons of silver buried in a cave in the desert. And I've met some men who are sure they can find it."

I gave her a quick kiss on her cheek and headed for the I-10 on-ramp a few blocks away. Entering the highway, I headed east.

"All right, honey, let's have the whole story."

She took a deep breath. "A few weeks ago I met this very

MY LIFE WILL NEVER BE THE SAME AGAIN

distinguished man at a swank dinner party. He's an archaeologist or something at the university. We got into a discussion and after I told him my ex-husband is pretty rich he said he could let me in on a terrific opportunity. A group of his friends are about to survey the desert to locate simply tons of Mexican silver coins. They've invented a gadget that can spot concentrations of metal though it's deep underground. They just need money to hire a helicopter to search miles of desert."

Frankly, I was skeptical. "Where did this silver originate?"

"San Diego. When Santa Ana was surrounding the Alamo, the Mexican government sent this wagon train loaded with silver coins, minted in San Diego, to pay the soldiers. The wagon train got lost in the desert. They ran out of food and water and the men began dying off. When only a few remained alive, and the horses used for food, they were forced to hide the silver in a cave in a canyon. Then they blew up the entrance. Only one man got through to tell Santa Ana what happened, and he died before he could tell where the silver was hidden."

"Sounds like a classic con to me," I laughed.

"That's because you have little faith," she retorted. "The professor showed me his credentials. He's very highly regarded."

. Ahead on the Interstate an information sign loomed up on the shoulder. REST AREA NEXT EXIT NO FACILITIES. I made a quick right turn and found myself in what was not much more than a hard-surfaced clearing. Numerous tire tracks led off from the clearing.

"Dirt bikers," I said to Tina. "This must be where they do their cross country wheelies on weekends. Let's follow the tracks for a few miles to see what's out there."

We drove on for nearly an hour, admiring the great variety of cacti and desert flowers. Tina tried to turn the conversation to treasure hunting but I put a finger to her lips.

"Let's just enjoy being together — like old times before you got

MY LIFE WILL NEVER BE THE SAME AGAIN

that crazy notion of divorce."

Her eyes blazed. "Divorce was not a crazy notion. I'm expanding my horizons. Don't try changing the subject. If you won't help me find the silver I'll get somebody who will."

We rode on in silence. I began to feel uneasy when, in the rear-view mirror, I noticed the sky darkening rapidly. "Uh, oh. We may be in trouble. Looks like a dust storm blowing up. We'd better turn back."

Before I could spin around, the sound of a siren brought me to a stop. A Border Patrol Jeep pulled alongside and an officer got out and approached my car.

"May I see your drivers' license, sir?"

I handed it to him. He studied it carefully and looked me over. "Your registration, please."

I removed it from the steering column and handed it to him. He checked it and his face broke into a grin. "New toy, eh?"

"Yes. Just got it yesterday. I'm giving it an off-road test."

"You picked a bad place and a bad time to do it. This area is swarming with illegal immigrants sneaking across the border. Besides, there's a big dust storm blowing up to the east. You'd better get out of the desert as soon as you can. I would advise that you not try to go back the way you came. Your best bet is to go down to Nogales and take Interstate Nineteen back to Tucson."

"How far is Nogales?"

"About twenty miles. Ten miles or so west of here you will come to a box canyon. Stay out of there or you could become lost and never be found. Follow the rim of the canyon south until you come to a dirt road. That road will take you to Nogales."

He returned to his Jeep. "I'm going back toward the storm to see if there are any other stragglers out here."

As the trooper left, Tina's face beamed. "Did you hear what he said? A canyon! I'll bet there's where the silver is."

MY LIFE WILL NEVER BE THE SAME AGAIN

I exploded. "For heaven's sake forget about treasure hunting. I just want to get us out of here alive."

We continued on, not speaking, until Tina pouted. "I'm hungry."

"I'm sorry, your ladyship, but I left the picnic hamper back at the castle. So thoughtless of me."

She didn't appreciate my levity.

We had driven for nearly half an hour after leaving the Border Patrol officer when we approached the entrance to a canyon. "This must be the one the trooper told us about," I said.

Tina suddenly sat up and pointed to a spot off to the right. "Look over there, Blake."

I followed her pointing finger. In the distance a plume of smoke rose skyward. "Could be some hikers or maybe a mine. Anyway, they might have something to eat."

As I pulled up to a bonfire blazing in a clearing I saw no one. Suddenly a large, sombrero-topped man holding a rifle stepped from behind a clump of mesquite. Two other men cautiously followed him. "Buenas dias, amigos," the big man greeted us, "so nize you come to our assistance."

A chill ran down my spine. "What the hell are you doing out here?"

The man shrugged. "We have had, what you call it? most unfortunate accident." He motioned for me to get out of my car and follow him.

Behind the mesquite, in a shallow gully, sat a dilapidated panel truck, one wheel off. "The axle, she break, " the man said.

He returned to my SUV and walked around it. "Nize car. Maybe we make trade."

"Trade for your old truck? You must be loco."

"But, amigo, my truck is — how you call it? — collector item.

MY LIFE WILL NEVER BE THE SAME AGAIN

Maybe worth much dinero." His companions guffawed loudly.

In the end he made me an offer I couldn't refuse. Make the trade or our bones would bleach under the desert sun. I opted for the trade.

The men quickly transferred several large burlap-wrapped bales from the truck.

"Marijuana," I whispered to Tina, "they're smugglers."

As my car disappeared in the distance, Tina spied something shiny lying in the sand. She picked it up and screamed "Blake, it's a Mexican silver peso! Those men are getting away with our treasure."

I took the coin from her and examined it, then burst out laughing. "Look at the date. This coin is only ten years old. One of those men must have dropped it."

She took it from me, threw it on the ground and stomped on it in anger. "I still think the old silver is hidden in that canyon."

In an attempt to make the best of a trying situation, I examined my new acquisition. "Look, honey," I called to Tina, "there's a pile of blankets in here. Those men must have been living in the van."

"I'm not sleeping on some filthy blankets."

I spread the blankets out and lay down. "Suit yourself, but it's going to get pretty cold tonight. And then there's the rattlesnakes..."

She leaped into the truck, lay beside me, and began shivering. "I'm scared."

I pushed the hair back from her face and gently kissed her forehead. "Don't be. We're safe here, and in the morning things will look a lot better."

Suddenly she threw her arms around me, her lips hungrily seeking mine. She pulled me closer. Closer...

The next morning the same Border Patrol officer who had stopped us the previous day picked us up and took us to Nogales. There we found my impounded SUV; the bandits had failed to elude

MY LIFE WILL NEVER BE THE SAME AGAIN

the authorities and were now guests of the U.S. government.

With the help of our rescuer we convinced the officials that we had in fact been carjacked and had no part in the smuggling operation. They released my vehicle and we headed home to Tucson.

Tina decided that the "real me" she searched for was the role of loving wife to a guy who truly adored her, so we remarried.

The treasure trove never existed, of course. A few days after our desert adventure the police arrested a trio of con men and charged them with bilking dozens of gullible people. I never told Tina that I tipped the bunco squad that a scam might be in progress.

Now when Tina gets that dreamy-eyed look and starts talking about some far-fetched scheme to make millions I just smile indulgently and hide the checkbook.

The piercing wail of a newborn infant shattered my reverie. A moment later a doctor stuck his head out of the delivery room door. "Congratulations, Mr. Ryan, you are the father of a fine baby boy."

Yes, my life will never be the same again.

LOVE IN FIVE SENSES

Her warm hand rests lightly on mine and the elusive fragrance of her perfume teases my memory. Did she wear the same one then?

On the large screen before us Humphrey Bogart is saying goodbye to Ingrid Bergman as the plane that will take her from him forever looms in the misty background.

Our decision to attend the Nostalgia Days Film Festival at our local theater had been a spontaneous and unanimous one. Now as we sit here the buttery taste of the popcorn from the bucket we share triggers a flood of pleasant recollections.

My heart skips a beat as I suddenly realize: I love her even more today than when we first saw *Casablanca* together so long, long ago.

THE FALL

In the sleepy little village of Rhymsville, the annual Seafood Festival was the grandest celebration of the year. In fact, for the hard-working, God-fearing people of the village it was the only festival of the year. For months the members of the Celebration Committee labored diligently, going over and over every minute detail to assure that this year's event would be the best ever.

When the big day arrived almost every man, woman and child from the settlement gathered in a meadow by the harbor, where gaily-bedecked pavilions dotted the landscape, and music filled the air.

As always, a Festival King and a Festival Queen had been chosen. To the surprise of no one, the most popular boy and girl in the high school, Jillian Smith and Jackson Jones, were named. Smiling broadly, they sat on two whalebone thrones mounted on a coral rock dais, to be crowned.

Mayor Bumble marched pompously up, placed intricately woven seaweed crowns bedecked with a myriad of tiny seashells upon their heads. With the tip of a harpoon, he touched each of them lightly on a shoulder and solemnly intoned "I now pronounce you King and Queen of this year's Seafood Festival." The assembled throng roared an accolade.

At that moment a spotter high atop the mast of a beached derelict schooner sang out:

"Shrimp boats are coming, their sails are in sight.
Shrimp boats are coming, there'll be feasting tonight."

The mayor strode to where a huge pot hung suspended above a stack of firewood. "I'll get the water hot so the shrimp can be steamed as soon as they are brought ashore." He looked into the pot and let out a bellow. "Who in tarnation is in charge of this pot? There's no water in it!"

THE FALL

The members of the Festival Committee looked at each other sheepishly.

"Don't worry, sir," Jackson spoke up, "there's a spring at the top of Makeout Hill. I'll run up there and get some water." He grabbed a bucket and started off.

"Wait," Jillian called. "I'll go with you."

Jackson's heart soared. For months he had tried to get Jillian up on Makeout Hill but to no avail. *She wants me* he exulted inwardly.

The path up the hill was steep and treacherous. Jackson placed an arm around Jillian's waist to steady her. Furtively, he let a hand slip up under her blouse. She removed it gently but he tried again. Again she pushed his hand away.

When they reached the top he could no longer control his passion. He dropped the pail, wrapped his arms around her and rained kisses on her lips.

"No, Jack," she whispered. "Not now, not here."

At that moment the loose gravel beneath their feet gave way and they tumbled head-over-heels down the hill.

When they rolled to a stop at the bottom, Jillian screamed "Jack, are you all right?"

He picked himself up, brushed himself off, then stooped to pick up the crown that had fallen from his head. "I'm okay, I think, but my crown is broken."

REFRAIN
(All together and not too loud)
*Jack and Jill went up a hill
to fetch a pail of water
Jack fell down and broke his crown
and Jill came tumbling after*

AFTER THE FALL
(A sequel)

Jack Jones had not finished breakfast on the morning following his ignominious fall down Makeout Hill when his doorbell rang. He opened the door to find a dapper man wearing a pinstripe suit and derby hat standing there.

"Jack Jones?" the man asked.

"Yes."

The man feigned an expression of incredulity. "Why are you not in the hospital, young man?" Pushing past Jack, he entered the room. "Don't you realize how serious the injuries from your fall might be?"

He presented a card. "I'm Phineas Phoggmaker, attorney-at-law, from the city of Philadelphia. As soon as I heard of your grievous fall I rushed here to offer my services to see that you and that sweet, innocent young lady (I'll talk with her later) who fell with you are properly compensated for the life-threatening trauma you suffered."

A grin broadened Jack's face. "Oh, she ain't all that innocent, Mr. Phoggmaker. Just last night after the festival we went back up..."

The lawyer stopped him. "You really don't remember clearly anything that happened after you fell. In your daze things you think you remembered happening were only fantasies of your fevered brain."

"Well, sir, if what happened was only a fantasy it was the granddaddy of all fantasies."

Phoggmaker quickly changed the subject. "Why did you go up the hill on the day of the festival?"

"To get a pail of water."

"What was the water for?"

"Well, Mr. Phoggmaker, the shrimp boats were coming and the

AFTER THE FALL

Festival Committee forgot to bring water to steam the shrimp."

"Aha! Negligence on the part of the committeemen. Now, who sent you up the hill?"

"Nobody sent me. I told Mayor Bumble that I would go get some water and I grabbed a pail and took off."

"Did the mayor try to stop you?"

"No, sir."

Phoggmaker shook his head gravely. "Worse case of dereliction of duty I ever heard of." He put an arm around Jack's shoulder. "Young man, you and Miss Jillian have ample grounds for a lawsuit, and I am here to offer my services..."

Because a muncipality was involved, the litigation was moved to Capitol City. The trial was short, the jury liberal. Finding for the plaintiffs: Actual and punitive damages in the amount of twenty-five million dollars.

When the verdict was read, Mayor Bumble stormed over to lawyer Phoggmaker. "You ambulance-chasing old coot, everything in the village wouldn't bring near that amount. I'll take this all the way to the Supreme Court. You'll rot in hell before you see a dime."

A pained expression crossed Phoggmaker's face. "Sir, you underestimate me. Do you think I would have taken this case if I had not known there would be ample funds to pay off the judgement? My dear sir, the people of your village live in the shadow of riches beyond their wildest comprehension."

Mayor Bumble's eyes narrowed. "What do you mean?"

"The hill, sir. The hill. Do you know who owns that hill?"

The mayor scratched his head. "I know that there was a big mining operation up there, but it closed down years ago. I don't know whether or not the mining company still owns it but I can check with the County Clerk's office."

AFTER THE FALL

"That won't be necessary, sir. I had my research assistant, Miss Megapeaks, check on it. The hill does, indeed, belong to the Eclipse Mining Company. These ruthless people have let what has become an attractive nuisance go unguarded in wanton disregard for the safety of life, limb and morals — yes, sir, I said morals — of the young people of your fair village.

"Do you have any idea, sir, of how many babies born in your village were conceived on that hill? Well, sir, I won't offend your own moral sensibilities by dwelling on the subject but it's a safe bet most of the firstborns were."

Phoggmaker took a handkerchief from his pocket and blew his nose loudly. "Has the mining company tried to keep the unwary boys and girls off this dangerous mountain? Do they have an electrified fence around it? Guard dogs patrolling the perimeter? Even warning signs? The answer to all is 'No'. They have done nothing to protect the good people of your fair village. The international industrialists who own that company must pay, and pay dearly, for their cavalier attitude. I'm proud to offer my services..."

EPILOGUE

As part of their settlement with Eclipse Mining, the village took title to Makeout Hill and built a ski resort there. The first person down the slopes crashed into a coral rock dais on which sat two whalebone thrones, and broke his neck. Fortunately, the village had liability insurance (underwritten by Caveat Insurers, a subsidiary of Eclipse Mining).

The injured man's legal action is being handled by Phineas Phoggmaker, Esquire, without the help of his research assistant Miss Megapeaks who, accompanied by Jack Jones and his multi-million-dollar settlement departed for Nashville, Tennessee, where she seeks a career as a country music singer.

AFTER THE FALL

Immediately after the accident on the ski slopes, Mayor Bumble disappeared. Coincidently, all the cash from the mining company settlement remaining in the village treasury disappeared at the same time.

Miss Jillian Smith is the mother of a healthy baby boy born nine months after the Seafood Festival. She declines to identify the father.

COORDINATE, MY DEAR, COORDINATE

The morning sun was beginning to climb into the sky as Sarah sat on a park bench idly kicking at loose rubble. *It won't be long before I'm out of this hick town.* She glanced at her watch. *Danny will be coming pretty soon.*

A woman came out of a shop across the street and began rolling down an awning stenciled FANNIE'S FASHIONS. Rainwater from the previous day's showers poured out as the awning opened, splashing the sidewalk. The woman gave Sarah a friendly smile then went back inside.

Sarah stood up and began walking down the settlement's one business street. After she passed the town limits her steps slowed and she looked expectantly down the road at a fast-approaching car. The car squealed to a stop and a man's voice shouted. "C'mon, shake a leg."

She scrambled in as the door swung open. "Gee, Danny, your disguise is so good even I wouldn't recognize you."

He handed her a long blonde wig, dark glasses, a form-fitting black sheath, and a flat, wide-brimmed hat. "Here's yours. Get it on before anybody sees you."

The transformation was made quickly. Danny started the car and put it in gear. "Did you make sure you were seen in town this morning?"

"Yeah. The old biddy at the dress shop saw me. Jim was going into the barber shop and he saw me. Mac was driving by and he waved to me."

Danny pursed his lips. "I'm sorry I couldn't let Mac in on this. He's been a good friend but he couldn't keep his mouth shut if he knew. Anyway, things are going just as we planned. They know you were in town days after I left, so they won't be looking for us

COORDINATE, MY DEAR, COORDINATE

together. By the time that stupid town marshal puts two and two together we'll be long gone."

Sarah smiled. "Yeah, gone from this dammed stuffy little town. Away from living in a crappy little house with none of the nice things we had before we came here."

"Sorry about that, kid. But you gotta admit it's been a good place to hide out after that last heist failed."

They drove slowly down Main Street. Jim, exiting the barber shop, called to Fannie. "Looks like the summer folks are arriving early. You got plenty of bonnets and hoop skirts in stock?"

"Oh stop your joshing, Jim. You know I carry only the latest fashions." She gazed at the passing car. "Never saw that pair before. Wonder where they're staying."

Jim leered. "That gal is a real looker. She'll turn a few heads."

Danny pulled into a parking place in front of the bank and he and Sarah stepped out. "We got to move fast. When I take care of the guard be ready to collect the cash."

Sarah hung a large beach bag over her shoulder and they strolled into the bank.

A cart loaded with currency to be distributed to the tellers was being pulled from the vault.

Danny sided up to the one security guard and prodded him with a gun barrel. Affecting a heavy European accent, he hissed "Make one sound and you gonna be dead. A sudden vicious blow with the gun barrel to the man's head dropped him.

"This is a stickup," Danny shouted. "Put all the money in the lady's bag. All loose bills. Rip the bands off. No dye packets, or somebody gets iced. Everybody cooperate real nice and nobody gets hurt."

With the bag filled, Danny and Sarah turned and ran toward the door. At that moment Fannie entered the bank. Immediately sensing something was wrong, she slumped to the floor as the bandits dashed

COORDINATE, MY DEAR, COORDINATE

past her.

"We did it," Sarah screamed in exhilaration as they sped away.

A short distance out of town Danny made a sharp turn onto a dirt road. He sped to a thick grove of trees hiding a large semi-trailer with its back door open and a ramp down. Without hesitation, he drove into the truck. Quickly he and Sarah jumped out and closed the truck door.

They hurredly stripped off their disguises. Danny put on a leather jacket, a fake mustache, dark sunglasses and a cowboy hat. "They'll be looking for a man and woman in a sports car, not a guy driving a big rig," he grinned. He gave Sarah a quick kiss. "Go back home through the woods. Stay off the road. Play it cool, honey. I'll send for you as soon as the heat's off."

Danny got into the truck and drove away. When he reached the paved road he turned and headed into town. The town marshal flagged him down. "Hey, buddy, did a black car pass you on the road?"

"Yeah, a sharp little sports job, goin' like a bat outta hell." He jerked a thumb over his shoulder. "Headin' east."

When Sarah trudged up to her modest cottage she saw the owner of the dress shop waiting at the gate.

"Did he leave you any of the money, dear?" Fannie greeted her. "He won't be coming back, you know."

A sudden fear gripped Sarah. "I - - I don't know what you mean," she stammered.

"The money you and Danny — I presume it was Danny — took from the bank. If he does elude the police, and I don't think he will for long, I doubt he'll include you in his future plans. It should go a lot easier with you if you turn yourself in and tell the authorities where Danny is going."

COORDINATE, MY DEAR, COORDINATE

Sarah frantically grasped at straws. "What makes you think I had anything to do with a bank robbery?" she demanded.

Fannie pointed at Sarah's feet. "The shoes gave you away, dear. They just didn't coordinate with that stunning outfit you were wearing. I wracked my brain trying to figure where I'd seen those shoes and suddenly it dawned on me. Just this morning you were sitting on a park bench kicking at lord knows what and I remember saying to myself 'that poor thing, deserted by her husband and probably down to that last pair of atrocious shoes. I must find a way to get her a new pair without offending her'."

She smiled."You see, dear, when you're in my business you tend to notice those things."

FORTUNE COOKIE ROMANCE

Wow, what a doll I thought when I caught sight of her sitting across the room from me. Long blonde hair, gorgeous figure. Why is she eating alone in a Chinese restaurant? I wonder. But, then, why am I?

It started in my mid-western home town. After a traumatic breakup with my girl friend I found myself obeying a horoscope's advice — You will find romance in an unexpected place. Go east, young man, go east.

I caught the next flight to Miami.

The cab from the airport took me to South Beach. Succumbing to the cabbie's impassioned plea that I book a room at a hotel of his choice, I checked in and went to my room. I noticed that the cab driver waited at the front desk for his referral fee.

Hey, everybody's got to make a living.

After a quick shower I felt refreshed but hungry. I went back down to the lobby.

"Where's a good place around here to eat?" I asked the desk clerk.

"Do you like Chinese?" he answered. "The Far East down the street has great food."

Far East, I mused, remembering the horoscope's advice, I can't go much farther east than that.

"Thanks," I said to the clerk, "I'll try it."

The Far East Chinese restaurant was not hard to find; the scent of exotic incense wafted from the doorway. I entered.

A diminutive Oriental waitress glided up as soon as I seated myself. She placed a cup of steaming green tea in front of me and then, almost as an afterthought, handed me a fortune cookie. I gave

FORTUNE COOKIE ROMANCE

her my order and she moved quietly away.

As I waited for my lunch to be served I idly cracked open the fortune cookie and removed the message it contained: Some day you will see that special someone across a crowded room.

Shades of *South Pacific*! I thought. I let my gaze sweep the room, which really wasn't all that crowded. Then I saw her, sitting alone.

The girl opened a fortune cookie, read the message, then looked over at me and smiled.

I gave a mental shrug. *What have I got to lose?* I picked up my cup of tea and walked over to her. "Hi, I'm Brent and you're beautiful, and I think you gave me a come-hither look."

She lifted her eyebrows slightly. "I'm Sybil and you're not bad looking yourself, but I was just amused at my cookie message when I glanced over at you."

"Oh? What did it say?"

"Some day you will see that special someone across a crowded room."

"No! That's weird. Mine said the same thing. They must be having a sale on that one today."

She motioned for me to sit down. I set my tea cup on the table, dropped into a seat opposite her, and gave her a bemused smile.

"Do you come here often?"

She gave a quick toss of her shoulders. "As a matter of fact, I do. I meet a lot of prospective clients here." She reached into her purse, removed a card, and handed it to me.

SYBIL
PERSONAL SERVICES
555-1234.

"My afternoon rate is one hundred dollars. All-nighter and weekender prices negotiable."

I jumped up. "I'm not much of an afternoon guy, Sybil, and the

FORTUNE COOKIE ROMANCE

other options sound a little rich for my blood. Thanks anyway."
 I picked up my cup of tea and hurried back to my table.
Identical fortune cookies! What are the odds? Suddenly came the dawn. *I wonder what commission the waitress gets?*
 Hey, everybody's got to make a living.

IT STARTED WITH A KISS

It started with a kiss. Annoyed at being awakened at three o'clock in the morning, I gently pushed her away. "Not now," I murmured.

She persisted, pressing her warm body against mine, nuzzling my neck and breathing softly into my ear.

Again I pushed her away, this time harder. She slipped off the bed and, with a loud thump, hit the floor.

Mouthing her own unique version of an expletive, she jumped back in bed and pounced on me, vehemently decrying my blatant lack of concern for her physical needs.

Groggily I lifted my legs over the side of the bed and groped for my slippers.

"Oh, all right, Precious," I growled, "If you really have to go out at this ungodly hour, come on."

With a sigh of resigntion I led my little dog to the door.

THE GIRL ON THE BUS

If you have never traveled cross-country by bus, your education has missed an important chapter in the textbook of human relations. Few other places offer the opportunity to become a spectator in the constantly changing parade of humanity that enters front and center, spends its allotted time in review, then passes on into oblivion.

Hiding behind a facade of apparent indifference, the bus passenger can observe unobtrusively the interplay between fellow passengers or, at will, interject himself into the minute dramas unfolding. Unlike with airline travel, where passengers often hide their faces behind walls of their own thoughts or the pages of in-flight magazines, and rarely exchange more than a few words with the person sitting next to them, perhaps the very tedium of a long bus ride fosters the development of a degree of camraderie among bus passengers.

Bus travelers run the gamut in personalities, from the cheerful and gregarious to the sullen and morose. A witty conversationalist may (heaven forbid!) be seated beside a boring dullard. Fortunately, unless the bus is crowded he usually has the option of moving in the hope of finding a more congenial seatmate. But behind each face, be it a warm, friendly one or a dour, sad or pathetic one lies a story begging to be told. Take my own for example.

What began as a pleasant motorhome tour of the west went terribly awry. Clashing personalities. Flaring tempers. A hasty retreat from a situation that to me had become untenable found me on a bus headed east.

If I had stopped to think at the time I would have realized that by bus from Montana to south Florida is a four-day journey, and I

THE GIRL ON THE BUS

would have endured the conflict aboard the Winnebago until we reached a city with an airport. But who stops to think at a time like this?

Viewed in retrospect, my Greyhound adventure was a kaleidoscope of images, prismatic glimpses into the lives of those whose paths crossed mine.

There was the black truck driver who sat down at my table when we stopped for lunch somewhere out on the plains. Forced by motor trouble, he had abandoned his truck on the road and was returning to his home base by bus.

Though he had made a living driving trucks most of his adult life, his great ambition was to be a preacher. He had had no formal religious training, he told me. In fact, he admitted, during his youth he had been something of a hell-raiser, drinking too much, gambling, fighting and womanizing. But now he had a burning desire to preach the Gospel, and he hungered for some small word of encouragement from a stranger at a remote bus stop.

Somewhere along the way a young Japanese student came aboard. He was seeing America on one of those unlimited-travel passes sold abroad to lure tourists to this country.

For hours we talked of travel, of politics, of religion and philosophy. Of a war fought in the dim past of his grandfather's time, a war that was to me still a grim and harsh reality.

Then there was the driver of a near-empty bus on a leg of the journey through rural Georgia who, despite a posted rule prohibiting drivers from conversing with passengers while the bus was in motion, spun a harrowing tale of the double life he once led, with a wife and family at one end of his run and a mistress at the other end.

But when I think back on my trip, my most cherished memory is the memory of a girl.

Somewhere south of Chattanooga she came aboard, glided down the aisle and settled into a seat across the aisle from where I sat. She was pretty, with dark shoulder-length hair and long lashes that sheltered deep blue-velvet eyes. She glanced in my direction and

THE GIRL ON THE BUS

favored me with a nod and a faint smile. A friendly one, I thought.

Idly my inquisitive mind began appraising the newcomer, drawing fantasy pictures as to who and what she was. With her fresh girl-next-door beauty and her apparent friendly nature, she could be a model, or she could work in public relations. She did not work outdoors, of that I was certain. The rose petal glow of her face showed none of the ravages of long exposure to a unrelenting sun, only the hint of occasional afternoons at the beach.

Did she work in an office? Her long, tapered fingers appeared capable of making music on a typewriter or a computer keyboard...or a piano. Was she a musician?

My mind continued to conjure up conjectural images. Could she be an executive? A lawyer? A doctor? Her casual travel attire of tastefully coordinated blouse and slacks offered no clue as to her economic or social status. No, I decided, executive and professional types rarely travel on an interstate bus.

I was munching on some peanuts when she came aboard. "Have some," I offered.

She smiled shyly and shook her head.

"They're low-cal," I quipped, though her trim figure belied the need of any dietary restrictions.

Her face beamed as she extended a cupped hand. The ice was broken.

"I've been visiting my children in Tennessee," she volunteered. Her voice was soft and cultured.

So she had children. At least two. She appeared to be in her mid-twenties so the children had to be quite young.

"They're living with their grandparents," she added.

She had not said "my parents" so it was evident the children were living with the parents of their father. What tragic episode in this girl's life led to her giving up her children? Was she widowed? Divorced? My earlier appraisal of her hands revealed that she wore no rings.

THE GIRL ON THE BUS

I touched briefly on the chain of events that brought me to this place at this time. Her face and her voice showed compassion. The 'curious' in me wanted to know more about this lovely stranger but the 'romantic' in me pleaded that some small aura of mystery be permitted to remain.

The miles and the minutes flowed swiftly as we chatted amiably, chuckled at shared jokes, marveled at the beauty of passing scenery, daring not to penetrate the thin veil that kept us from being more than, by fateful chance, fellow travelers.

Then, just outside of Atlanta, with a farewell wave of her hand, she was gone. The delicate fragrance of her perfume lingered behind.

Life deals us far too few brief interludes of simple pleasures, but of these are memories made.

Who was the girl on the bus? I'll never know. I didn't ask her name.

SECOND CHANCE

Brilliant streaks of lightning knifed open the dark night, each flash giving birth to booming thunder that shook the dilapidated old building. Wind-driven rain assaulted the porous roof, dripping icy water on the frightened refugees from the civil violence in Rwanda huddled in the cavernous interior.

"Do you think somebody will find us?" Ellie gasped through chattering teeth. "Do you think anyone knows where the plane crashed?"

Brian's reassuring hug required no words.

The passengers who had escaped before the plane exploded bunched around two small fires that gave off a flickering light but little heat; the Africans, all Tutsi tribesmen, around one and the Americans and Europeans around the other.

Brian stood up. "I know all of you are scared and miserable and that many of you lost loved ones in the crash. But you're a lot better off here than if you had remained in Kigali." He paused. "And a helluva lot better off than those unfortunate ones who didn't get out of the plane."

"Do you know where we are?" one of the Europeans asked.

"We were near the border when that missile hit us and I'm pretty sure we came down in Uganda. Whoever shot us down is unlikely to come over here to look for us. Our people in Kampala know our flight plan, and when we don't show up on schedule they'll send out a search party. We're lucky we found this old barn, for what little protection it gives us. We're at a pretty high altitude so I'm guessing we're on an abandoned coffee plantation."

"Are there any villages near here?" another man asked.

SECOND CHANCE

Brian shook his head. "I doubt it. According to the handbook I was given when I was assigned to fly relief flights out of Kigali, this is pretty rough mountainous country. I was lucky to spot a flat area to put the plane down. Our main concern right now is that the area is infested with bands of wild-animal poachers, mostly Hutus from the Rwanda side of the border. They can be ruthless. Don't worry, we're going to get out of this."

He sat down beside Ellie, removed his jacket and placed it around the shivering girl's shoulders. "I didn't get a chance on the plane to ask why you're in Africa. What the hell are you doing here, anyway?"

"I'm a volunteer with the United Nations World Food Program."

Brian gave a hollow laugh. "Same old Ellie. Did you leave a lonely man behind this time, too? That's what led to our divorce, you know."

She glared at him."I divorced you because I found you were cheating on me with a flight attendant. You didn't even contest the divorce."

"You were always off saving the whales or something. I know my job took me away from home a lot, but when I was home you weren't. When I needed someone you weren't there. She was. You were cheating on me, too, but in a different way." Ellie looked down at the floor. "Are you going to marry her?"

A long moment passed before Brian answered softly. "She didn't get out of the plane, Ellie."

Ellie's eyes opened wide in horror. "Oh God, no! The stewardess on our plane was the one you were involved with? She pushed me off the plane but she didn't get off." She looked sharply at Brian. "You told her I was your ex, didn't you? She knew who I was but she saved my life anyway."

"She was doing what she was trained to do, saving as many

SECOND CHANCE

passengers as possible. Her luck ran out."

Ellie glared at him. "How did you get saved? I thought the captain was always the last one to leave a doomed ship."

"That's unfair, Ellie," he retorted angrily. "The plane broke in two when it hit the ground. The nose section skidded a distance from the rest of the plane. I managed to free myself from the wreckage and was running toward the burning cabin when the plane exploded. I almost tripped over you lying where you passed out. I picked you up and brought you in here."

She began sobbing. "I'm sorry. That was cruel of me. You must be hurting inside. I shouldn't have said it. I'm cold and I'm scared and I'm all mixed up."

Suddenly one of the Africans stood up and motioned for silence. He approached Brian. "Someone is outside. I will see who it is."

"Careful," Brian warned, "If it's poachers they might kill you."

The Tutsi gave a wry smile. "If it's Hutus they will kill all of us." He slipped out into the stormy night.

After what seemed like an eternity to the frightened survivors he returned.

"It's a Uganda Park Service patrol. They saw the flames and came to investigate. There is a dirt road leading up from the valley. They have radioed for trucks to come for us."

Brian grasped the African's hand. "Where did you learn to speak such perfect English?"

The man shrugged. "I was a professor at the university in Butare. I teach English."

Ellie clung to Brian's arm. "What happens after we get out of here?" she asked anxiously. "I mean, with you and me. What's going to happen to us?"

He gave her a tight hug. "Sometimes the Gods of Fate grant a second chance."

EULOGY FOR A FRIEND

December 11, 1995. A small detachment of U.S. Marines, vanguard of a force of 20,000 American military personnel, arrived in Bosnia. A fierce winter storm dumped three feet of snow on Buffalo, New York. In California, a sinkhole swallowed a multi-million-dollar mansion. The Miami Dolphins defeated the Kansas City Chiefs in a Monday Night football game.

Our little dog, Precious, died.

Tears flowed freely that night. Tears of mothers, fathers, husbands and wives whose loved ones were off to face unknown perils in a war-ravaged land. Tears of cold, hungry victims of the storm. Tears of frustration at the loss of a home. Tears of joyous exultation by Dolphin fans and bitter tears shed by the losers.

Unashamed tears from the eyes of two Golden Agers at the loss of a lovable, furry, four-footed friend.

Precious was never a healthy dog. The day we got her, at age six weeks, we rushed her to the vet when blood was detected in her stool. The doctor told us that if she lived through the night she would recover. She lived.

Throughout her life, Precious had a breathing problem. A short romp across a room left her panting hard. But the words "company coming" made her dance with joy. Precious loved people.

Our little Maltese dog was a finicky eater. No amount of coaxing would get her to down dry dog food. She would eat, grudgingly, only one kind of canned food — Mighty Dog Gourmet Dinner. But she loved turkey (white meat preferred), baked chicken, and roast beef. The word "cookie" brought her running, tail wagging.

Precious did not like taking a bath but she loved being clean. After being bathed, blow-dried, brushed and combed she became as

EULOGY FOR A FRIEND

frisky as a fawn on a spring morning.

When she wanted to, Precious displayed a remarkable degree of intelligence. When she didn't want to do your bidding she could be a master at looking stupid. Perhaps that was a display of intelligence. She didn't scratch at the door or bark when she had to "go". She just put her paws on the knee of a chosen servant and looked up imploringly. If the situation were urgent she might emit a soft woofing sound.

She knew most of the regular visitors to our home by name. One of my friends, Bob, always came around back to the door of my rec room. If Precious heard "Bob's coming" she would race to that door. On hearing "Uncle Harvey is coming", or "Company's coming", she would wait patiently by the front door.

Precious loved people.

As with all pets, Precious was a lot of trouble. She restricted our movements. Whenever we went out we had to hurry home to take care of her needs. If we traveled, there was the problem of what to do with Precious.

She had the annoying habit of getting us up at all hours when she had to pee-pee or poo-poo. And there were those anxious moments whenever she became sick.

Oh how we'll miss all that trouble.

Precious was only four years old.

BACK TO THE BEGINNING

"We are now making our final approach to Honolulu," the voice coming from the plane's speaker was warmly impersonal. "Please take your seats, lock all seat backs and tray tables in upright position, and fasten your seat belts. Turn off all electronic devices. Beverage service is now ended as flight attendants must prepare cabin for landing. We hope you have enjoyed your flight, and thank you for flying Delta."

With a twinge of sadness, Marla remembered the first time she heard that announcement. She was sitting in the same seat then, 16A, with Derek beside her. Tall, suave, handsome Derek, the embodiment of every woman's wildest fantasies. At least that is what she thought when they first met, Marla recalled bitterly. But it was over now. Ended. Kaput. Except for one bit of unfinished business.

Marla's thoughts drifted back to the day Derek first walked into the office where she had just began working, the heartbeat-skipping moment she first laid eyes on him.

"Who's the Adonis?" she whispered to the woman at the next desk.

Carole frowned. "Derek Dunn. He's a friend of the boss but stay away from him. He's hit on every girl in the office."

"Including you?" Marla teased.

"Yeah, including me." She busied herself with some work. "Don't say I didn't warn you."

Derek appeared not to notice Marla that first day, nor the second time he came into the office, but a week later he walked up to her desk and placed on it a slim vase holding one rose. "One perfect

BACK TO THE BEGINNING

American Beauty rose for one perfect American beauty." he smiled. Bending over, he picked up her hand and kissed the back of it gently. He then turned and entered the inner office.

Marla's pulse raced and she could feel her ears reddening. Carole's sharp voice snatched her back into reality.

"God's gift to women is starting to make his move," she sniffed. "The stinker probably checked with Personnel to see if you're married. When he comes back out of the boss'es office he's going to put a hit on you."

Sour grapes, Marla thought. *So Derek and Carole had something going and it didn't work out. Hell hath no fury...*

Derek did ask her for a date, and to her own amazement she accepted. *Moth and the flame?* Maybe, she thought.

Carole grinned and began humming the theme from *Dragnet.*

Their first evening together was Cinderella-perfect — dinner at a fine restaurant, then a long drive along the ocean in his convertible, with nothing but stars between them and infinite space.

Dexter was the personification of Sir Lancelot the entire evening, but when they returned to her apartment he started to follow her inside. She stopped him.

"Not tonight, Derek. I have to get to the office early in the morning for a conference and I need to get a good night's sleep."

His face mirrored his disappointment. "You can't put me off forever, Marla." He turned to leave and called back over his shoulder. "I'll pick you up for dinner tomorrow at seven." Not "May I pick you up?" or "Will you have dinner with me?". Just a blunt foregone conclusion. Self-assurance or arrogance? Marla asked herself. Arrogance, she decided later. Definitely arrogance.

When they returned home the next evening Derek was bolder. "You are going to invite me in for a nightcap, aren't you?"

BACK TO THE BEGINNING

Marla's heart pounded and her fingers trembled as she inserted the key in the lock. *Things are moving too fast. Better put on the brakes.* But she beckoned him in.

Derek stood over her as she fixed two drinks. After they sat down on a sofa he slowly and deliberately placed his glass on a coffee table and reached to take Marla into his arms.

Startled, she jerked back, spilling some of her drink. She jumped up and began furiously brushing the liquid from her dress. "I think you got the wrong impression of me, Derek," she blurted out.

He stood up, a hard smile on his face. "Oh, I don't think so. Marla. You and I were made for each other and you know it." He repeated his admonition of the previous night. "You can't put me off forever."

With an impatient sigh, he started toward the door. "I'll pick you up tomorrow at the usual time."

"No, Derek, not tomorrow." Marla's voice bordered on panic. "Call me next week."

In the days that followed, Marla prayed alternately that he would call or that he wouldn't call. But she knew that if he did call she was ready to do whatever he wanted. *The Year 2000 is coming up, the dawning of a new century. It's time I get in step with the world.* She went to a drug store, had a long-held prescription filled, and swallowed the first pill from a dial-shaped container. When his call did come she was thrown into a dilemma.

"Marla," his voice was firm, crisp. "I'm flying out to Hawaii on business and I want you to go with me. I've arranged with your boss to give you a week off. Be ready by nine tomorrow morning." He hung up.

So, this is it. I play the cards Derek deals or leave the game. When Derek arrived the next morning she was packed and ready.

"You look like you're taking enough clothing to last a month,"

BACK TO THE BEGINNING

she observed as he placed her suitcase in the trunk of his car. A masculine, folded garment bag lay beside a large, wheeled pink luggage piece, the kind a woman might choose.

"I'm taking some merchandise samples to our Honolulu agent," he shrugged.

On the flight to Hawaii, Derek was the ever-attentive charmer, allaying with gentle caresses and frequent libations from the plane's bar, her fear of flying over water.

When they checked in at the hotel on arrival, the desk clerk gave Derek a sly wink. "You're in Room seven- eleven, Mr. Dunn. That must be your lucky number."

Marla sensed uneasily that Derek had been here before, more than once.

In their room, Marla showered and slipped into the sexy black negligee saved especially for this moment. Dexter was already undressed and lying on the bed when she came out of the bathroom. He lifted his arms toward her. Moving almost as in a trance, she fell into his embrace, head swimming, heart pounding, breath coming in short, ecstatic gasps. In one searing moment, twenty-six years of virginity ended.

When it was over, Derek was visibly annoyed. "I never deflowered a virgin before," he grumbled. "It was not all that pretty. I hope you had sense enough to protect yourself." He got up, walked out onto the balcony overlooking the sea, and lighted a cigarette.'

Marla remained in bed, sobbing softly.

Derek was not one to remain angry for long, especially when there was a desirable female available. A while later he returned to bed and took her in his arms.

This time it was as she had always dreamed it would be, the way it screamed from the pages of countless paperback romance novels.

BACK TO THE BEGINNING

The business matter that brought Dexter to Hawaii was dispatched quickly. A stocky Oriental man wearing dark sunglasses appeared at the door. He handed Dexter a thick envelope and left with the pink suitcase.

Reckless, fun-filled days of sun, sea, sand and sightseeing quickly dispelled Marla's traumatic memories of that first time. A breathless climb to a mountaintop, where only Derek's strong arms saved her from a potential fall. A moonlight-bathed luau where the sensuous dancing and enchanting music of native Hawaiians wove a magical tapestry of romance. And in the nights another "s" was added. — sex. Vibrant, exciting, passionate lovemaking. For Marla, the week ended far too soon.

When Marla returned to the office, Carole met her with a cold stare. "I hear you spent the week in Hawaii with Derek. Lottsa luck, kid."

Marla fumed inwardly. *Does everything that happens around here become common knowledge?*

Only a few days passed before Derek dropped another bombshell. "I have to make a delivery in San Francisco. We'll leave Friday night and be back Sunday. You won't have to take time off from work."

"But Derek, I haven't rested up from Hawaii yet..."

"Be packed and ready to leave when you get off from work Friday," he interrupted. He hung up.

Delivery? Delivery of what? Marla thought frantically. *He's taking me for granted. He's trying to dominate my life. That dammed maddening arrogance of him.*

But she was ready when he picked her up. She noticed, with a fleeting flash of alarm, another large pink suitcase lay beside his

BACK TO THE BEGINNING

overnight bag in the car trunk.

    More "demand" trips came in the ensuing weeks. Marla could feel the resentment growing. But there was another disturbing stirring within her that she feared was more physical than emotional. Her gynecologist confirmed the most devastating of her fears.

    "There's no question about it, Marla," she said gently. "You're pregnant."

    "But you told me the pill is safe." Tears welled up in Marla's eyes.

    "When did you began taking them?" The doctor's furrowed brow reflected her concern.

    "About a week before..." Marla's voice trailed off.

    Dr. Bowen could not conceal her exasperation. "Marla, I explained to you that you have to take them for at least a month before you could be considered safe. Didn't you understand me? Even then, the pill is only about ninety-five percent effective. Within a year, five out of a hundred women using only the pill for contraception will become pregnant."

    Marla left the office in a daze. *Derek will have to be told. How will he take the news?*

    At an intimate candlelight dinner in her apartment she finally summoned the courage to tell him. He leaped to his feet in a rage.

    "How could you be so dammed stupid? I won't have a wife and kid fouling up my life. No way! You'll have to get rid of it." He stormed from the apartment, slamming the door violently.

    She would not see him again.

    Two tormented nights later as Marla tossed in a fitful sleep, the insistent ringing of her telephone roused her. Half asleep, she picked up the receiver. Carole was on the line, her voice verging on hysteria.

    "Marla, I just heard on the late news that Derek has been

BACK TO THE BEGINNING

arrested for drug trafficking. I'm scared. I took trips with him, too."

It was all too clear, now Marla realized. Derek had no real feeling for her or for Carole. He just needed a woman companion to mask the real purpose of his trips *Those dammed pink suitcases. The kind a woman would choose!*

Stunned, Marla could only gasp. "I don't know what we can do, Carole. If we do become involved we'll have to pray the authorities will understand."

With the dawning of a new day, Marla knew what she had to do. A few telephone calls took care of necessary arrangements.

Being assigned seat 16A on the flight to Hawaii was an incredible coincidence, but she had insisted on Room 711 when she made the hotel reservation. "Sentimental reasons," she told the travel agent.

The light bump of the landing gear against concrete as the plane touched down and rumbled along the runway snapped Marla from her reverie. The speaker came alive again. "Please remain in your seats until the plane has come to a full stop at the gate and the captain has turned off the seat belt sign. Then gather any personal belongings you have brought aboard and prepare to deplane. Please be careful when retrieving items from overhead compartments as they may have shifted in flight. Aloha! Enjoy your visit to Hawaii."

"Aloha," Marla thought grimly. The Hawaiian word meant both "hello" and "goodbye". How ironic. She quickly left the plane, brushed aside the smiling lei-bestowing hula girls greeting the passengers, and hailed a cab.

The ride from the airport to Waikiki was as beautiful as she had remembered it, except that the breathless anticipation of the previous trip was missing.

BACK TO THE BEGINNING

She checked in at the hotel desk and, disdaining the service of a bellboy, took an elevator up. The one small piece of hand luggage she carried required no help. *I won't need many clothes this time* she thought wryly as she packed for the trip.

Room 711 was just as she had remembered it. She took a long look at the bed she and Derek had shared, then stripped off her clothes and stepped into the shower.

She emerged nude and danced lightly around the room. "You should see what you're missing, Derek," she sang out. "You dirty bastard, you should see what you are missing."

She slipped into the filmy negligee she had first worn for Derek and carefully smoothed out all wrinkles. Almost mechanically, she walked out onto the balcony.

For interminable minutes, white-knuckled fingers gripping the metal railing, Marla stared down at giant waves crashing against the rocky shore. She and Derek had watched sunrises from here, shared goodnight kisses. "What a perfect place for a lovers' leap," they had joked. A few seconds of sheer terror and then... Oblivion!

Suddenly she stepped back and dropped to her knees, her body wracked with uncontrollable sobs. "Damn it, Derek," she screamed, "You're not worth it. You're just not worth it."

As soon as she could regain her composure she went back into the room. *I'm in control of my life, now!* She picked up the telephone and tapped in a number given to her by a freedom-of-choice group.

"Dr. Odaki? This is Marla Warren. I spoke to you by telephone from New York. Can you take care of that matter we discussed? I'm at the Seasprite Hotel, Room seven-eleven. Yes, I know that a hotel room is not the most conventional place to perform an abortion but that's the way I want it." She paused. "This is where it began so it's only fitting that it end here."

FIRE!

Fire! The lieutenant's sharp command broke the eerie silence Conrad's finger tightened on the trigger. So this was the moment of truth. Since his first day in the army the thought had tormented him. *When the time comes, will I be able to kill?*

Through the grueling days of basic training the thought seldom left his mind. Then on the voyage overseas when the convoy came under enemy air attack he huddled below deck with thousands of other men as the ship trembled to the pom-pom-pom of its anti-aircraft guns. He felt no fear, just relief. *At least I'm not up there shooting at other human beings.*

The attack ended as quickly as it began, the enemy planes driven off. Word drifted down to the men below: no casualties aboard. Some enemy aircraft fell, but this ship's gunners were not certain whether their shells, or fire from other vessels, got them.

Through the long night the Americans had been lying there—waiting. There was no doubt but that hostile soldiers were approaching, and a deadly ambush awaited them.

Dawn was breaking when shadowy figures began emerging from the woods, moving cautiously toward Conrad's platoon.

"Fire," The command echoed in Conrad's head. He closed his eyes and pulled the trigger. Again, and again, and again...

DICKENS WOULD TWIST IN HIS GRAVE

My all-time role model writer is Charles Dickens, but even in the best of my times or the worst of his times I could not hope to emulate this undisputed master of the English language so I must default (that's computerese for letting the computer do whatever it wants to when you don't have a clue as to how to recover the file you want) to my favorite contemporary author — Dave Barry.*

Why Dave Barry? He's funny. He's witty. He's irreverent. He can get away with literary murder and make the reader beg for more..

I will not try to take one of his situations and rewrite it, but I will attempt to do my version of a typical Dave Barry column.

IN HARM'S WAY — by Dave Barryless

I am constantly amazed at what gets into the newspaper (I'm amazed MY COLUMN gets into the newspaper). If you can believe this little tidbit spotted by an alert reader (me), you have to agree that the right-to-lifers have gone a tad too far. Does a HURRICANE have a right to live? I'm not making this up! The article days "Tropical Storm Bertha formed Friday in the far eastern Atlantic Ocean, on a westward trek keeping it temporarily out of harm's way."

Are they implying that if Bertha comes too close to Florida's shore some mean old men — oops! mean old persons — will dump zillions of iodide crystals into her vortex, making her pee-pee all of her energy into the Gulf Stream (not to be confused with Gulfstream Park, where men and women, and persons whose sexual orientation could go either way, poop away millions of dollars every day of the racing season betting on horses that know if they want to stay out of harm's

205

DICKENS WOULD TWIST IN HIS GRAVE

way — namely a one-way trip to the glue factory — they had better at least make a stab at winning)?**

Anyway, as those of you who aren't still hiding in hurricane shelters know, Bertha skirted our shore and went on to the Carolinas where Southern hospitality dictates that all of God's creatures, large or small, be made welcome.

No one warned Bertha that she might be in harm's way and let her smash her guts out against some old (fully-insured) fishing piers (There's a quaint saying in the South that when a structure covered by insurance placed with a Northern insurance is destroyed by storm, fire or whatever, it has been "sold to the Yankees").

You read a lot about "mad cow" disease. The maddest cow I ever saw was one who hadn't been milked in a long time. Her udder drooped so low she kept stepping on it. Talk about mad! Poor old bossie found it utterly impossible to keep her udder out of harm's way.

A final story — honestly I'm not making this up — is about a freak accident that happened deep in the heart of Texas.

A woman heading from Arizona to Florida on Interstate 10 swerved to avoid hitting a skunk crossing the road. She lost control of her car and ran into a stone wall, totaling her car and putting herself and a passenger in the hospital.

Two weeks later they left the hospital, got another car, and decided to return to Arizona. Eleven miles from home they smashed into a deer crossing the road, seriously damaging the car and terminating the deer. (By sheer coincidence, a restaurant near the crash site began offering venison on its menu that same night.)

The skunk involved in the first accident probably is still running. However, if you should drive past that site keep your windows up and don't inhale.

Some way must be found to let animals know that when they cross highways they're putting themselves in harm's way.

DICKENS WOULD TWIST IN HIS GRAVE

In conclusion, whether or not you believe everything you read in your newspaper, don't even think about canceling your subscription. If the paper loses too many readers it might have to cut back on expenses. The editors could even drop my column, putting ME in harm's way. I would have to go to work for a living.

* Sentence has 73 words — a new personal record.
** 103 words! I just broke my old record.

UNANSWERED PRAYERS

"Oh, Great Allah," the bearded, turbaned man boomed, "wreak your vengeance on these infidels who surround me."

The gaunt-faced man fell to his knees. "Almighty Jehovah, Lord of Hosts, though sorely have I sinned, reveal now thy forgiving grace. Grant me the means to depart this evil place that I might devote my life to spreading the true Gospel."

"Blessed Mary, Mother of Jesus," cried the man in the long black frock, "come to the aid of your faithful servant."

The slight, brown-skinned man began chanting "Vishnu, Vishnu, Vishnu, most benevolent of gods, do not desert this humble person now."

Around its circular course the small white ball whirred and then dropped — into double zero.

ONE SMALL STEP FOR WOMANKIND

As Global Airlines Flight 613 swept low over the desert on its approach to Abu Dhama International Airport I could only marvel at the changes since my first visit to this tiny Persian Gulf emirate twenty years earlier.

Below me, hundreds of acres of oil storage tanks spread back from the harbor area. Miles of pipelines snaked across the desert floor to disappear in the shimmering haze beyond the horizon. The reflected gold of the setting sun transformed the pipes into yellow brick roads leading into an Oz-like city of gleaming glass and aluminum office buildings, domed mosques, and graceful minarets.

The contrast between the panorama unfolding below me, and the Abu Dhama I visited so many years ago B.O. before oil — was startling.

I'm Molly Mason, and I'm on my last assignment for the weekly-televised *Today's World* news magazine before I take over as anchor of the evening news in the fall. Oh, I deserve my new job. I've served my time in the trenches. But it was with smug satisfaction that I accepted, as the first woman ever on my network, the prestigious position long a male domain.

A few days ago the producer of *Today's World* called me into his office, "Molly, I want you to go film a segment on the Persian Gulf crisis as seen from Arab women's point of view."

I chose Abu Dhama as my base of operations as its history and development closely paralleled that of Iraqi-invaded Kuwait. And then I was curious. How much had it changed since I was there before?

That first trip was a high school graduation gift from ever-supportive parents. "Molly," my dad beamed as he handed me the tickets, "if you have your mind set on being a photo-journalist you

ONE SMALL STEP FOR WOMANKIND

might as well learn what remote parts of this old globe look like. As long as you stay with your tour group you should be perfectly safe."

The package was billed as a "Glamorous Arabian Nights Adventure", but after the glories of ancient Egypt and the passage through the canal, the "exotic ports-of-call" south of Suez were one disappointing sun-drenched sand dune after another. Abu Dhama proved to be no exception.

So choked with sand was the Abu Dhama harbor that only small native sailing dhows could enter. Our cruise ship anchored off the harbor mouth and we were ferried ashore.

A florid-faced, profusely perspiring Englishman, Her Majesty's official presence in this remote outpost of the British Commonwealth, hurried to the landing to greet us. He conducted us on a sightseeing tour of the town, which didn't take long as there was little to see along the dusty streets lined with mud or sheet metal buildings.

Of course, the inevitable bazaars selling native crafts beckoned to the gullible. Some members of our group headed for these shops to try their hopelessly outclassed bargaining skills on the merchants, wily men of the desert descended from generations of camel traders.

I had already accumulated far too much junk, and the joys of haggling for price no longer held any allure. Quietly I separated myself from the group and wandered aimlessly about.

The few women I saw on the streets, always accompanied by a man, wore flowing robes that covered them from head to foot, with only tiny slits for them to see through. They hurried past me, eyes downcast lest the very sight of this infidel girl in pith helmet, white blouse and khaki shorts damn their souls to eternal purgatory. *Damn, I thought,* my latent women's lib tendencies fully aroused, *this is no way for women to have to live.*

The ultimate insult came later.

"The ruling sheik has invited the men in your party to visit him at his palace," the British official informed us. "I must ask you ladies to

ONE SMALL STEP FOR WOMANKIND

remain here," he added nervously. "It is the custom."

He led us into a goatskin pavilion where we were invited to recline on camel hair carpets and be entertained by a small ensemble of native musicians playing strange woodwind and stringed instruments. They appeared not to be happy at playing for women.

My temper rose with indignation, but one of the older ladies put her arm around my shoulders and cautioned "Remember, dear, when in Rome..."

I couldn't wait to get out of Abu Dhama, though I expected our next stop, Saudi Arabia, to be no better.

But Saudi Arabia was to provide the one breathless madcap moment in my trip.

When we arrived at the port of Ad Dammam we were advised that all women going ashore, Muslim and non-Muslim, were required to wear the traditional abaya, a loose-fitting garment that covered the body from head to foot. The ship had a supply of these to lend.

For Western women, a headpiece was optional, but for a scheme hatching in my head I went all the way, including a hood that allowed only my eyes to show.

From Ad Dammam we took a grueling five-hour train ride to Riyadh, the Saudi capital city.

A small fleet of mini-vans met our group at the railroad and whisked us to our hotel. I quickly learned that the driver of my van was an American-educated young Saudi who spoke fluent English.

"Why don't I see women drivers?" I asked him.

"Muslim women do not drive," he answered.

"Why don't they?" I demanded, though I already knew the reason.

"Muslim women are not permitted to operate motor vehicles. It is the law of Islam."

I glared at him. "And I don't suppose women can vote in elections, either?"

ONE SMALL STEP FOR WOMANKIND

He shrugged. "If women were allowed to vote they would only vote as their fathers or husbands told them to."

Inwardly I seethed. *I can't do anything about the voting but about that driving thing...*

We arrived at the hotel late in the day and were assigned rooms. Afterward we assembled for dinner.

"Tomorrow," the Tour Director addressed us, "We will go on a sightseeing tour of the city. Be in front of the hotel by nine. Now I know we are all exhausted from the train ride so I suggest we turn in after dinner and get a good night's sleep." He added with a wry grin "There's no night life here to speak of."

The next morning I left the hotel a few minutes early and approached the first mini-van in line. The driver was the same one I had ridden with the previous day. He gave me a friendly smile.

"All ready to see the wonders of our city?"

As he opened the car door for me I gave him a quick shove that sent him reeling off balance. I jumped into the driver's seat, started the engine and roared off down the street.

At an intersection, a policeman was directing traffic. He glanced at me and gave a sudden double-take. His eyes opened wide and he began waving his arms wildly and blowing his whistle furiously. All traffic came to a stop.

My eyes smiled at him as I gave a little wave of my hand and took off, tires squealing.

At the next corner I made a sharp right turn, then ducked into an alley that ended behind the hotel where I was staying. *A blow for women's lib,* I exulted.

Leaving the mini-van there, I ran to the front of the hotel where the driver was talking excitedly to the tour group.

"Your car is back there," I called to him as I brushed past and headed for my room. "I've decided not go sightseeing today."

ONE SMALL STEP FOR WOMANKIND

I dashed into my room, locked the door and threw myself onto the bed, heart pounding. Then I broke into an uproarious laugh. *The look on that cop's face!*

After the Arabian trip I returned home, got my college degree in communications, and began the tedious climb up the ladder in my chosen profession.

As the plane came in for a landing I could see there had been tremendous physical changes in Abu Dhama since my first visit. But had social changes kept pace? I wondered.

Great visible improvements in the status of Arab women delighted me as I walked through the terminal. Everywhere efficient-looking dark-skinned women bustled about, some even giving orders to male associates. *Wonderful!*

Many of these women, I knew, were Pakistanis. But in an impromptu interview, one told me proudly "I am Arab, as are many of the other women working here." With flashing eyes she added "We will never go back to the old ways."

Riding in a Mercedes taxi along a broad palm-lined boulevard from the airport to my hotel I leaned back, closed my eyes and let my thoughts drift back to my girlhood visit to Arabia. Would I experience anything on this trip to equal the thrill of my madcap dash through the streets of Riyadh? Not likely, I thought. After all, this is a new Araby.

And, I had to admit with a resigned sigh, I am an older and, I hope, saner Molly Mason.

HIDING IN PLAIN VIEW

Tex took a sip from his beer and slowly shook his head. "It's hard to believe those terrorists were living right here among us and nobody had a clue."

"What do you mean 'were' living here?" Dave retorted, "I'll bet a month's pay they're still around."

"What makes you so sure?"

"Well, did you know there's a 'safe house' right here in this city where they can come and go and nobody will say a word?"

"You're nuts. Where is this safe house?"

"The public library."

"Now I know you're bullshitting me."

Dave shook his head. "Nope, it's something called 'confidentiality laws'. A librarian can't reveal any information about who uses the library, the books they read, or anything. A librarian in the next county was reprimanded because she told the FBI she had seen the nine-eleven terrorists using the computer there."

"That's ridiculous!"

"Yeah, it sure is. A few nights ago a representative of a national librarians association was on one of those talking heads news shows. The host asked her if she saw a known terrorist in her library, a person she knew was on the most-wanted list, would she call the FBI. I thought the news guy would have apoplexi at her reply."

"Yeah? What did she say?"

"She said no, that the terrorists have as much right to confidentiality as everyone else.."

Again Tex shook his head. "Them dammed liberals are ruining this country. Anyway, the terrorists can't do much without money. When we get bin Laden they'll have nobody to bankroll them and they'll dry up on the vine."

HIDING IN PLAIN VIEW

Pete chimed in. "Getting bin Laden won't be easy. I hear that he and his gang have enough food, water, ammo, and everything else they need to hod out in those caves for years."

Bob had sat quietly listening to the exchange between his friends. "I don't think we have to worry about bin Laden. He's dead."

"Hey, what makes you think that?" Tex asked.

"You know how long we waited before we started bombing those caves? I figure it's because we had a Delta Force team in there looking for him. Those Delta guys are tough and they're mean. They found him, slit his throat, and left him for his boys to find him. Nobody knows we got him, so they can't make a martyr of him. And they'll go nuts trying to decide which warlord turned on him and iced him. Those Afghan warlords change sides quicker than a rattler can strike."

"You may be right," Dave shrugged, "but I still think he's hiding in the library."

AGNU'S RUN

The moon was high in the sky when a weary Agnu, the gnu, staggered into an all-night tavern and plopped himself onto a stool. The bartender eyed him suspiciously.

"I ain't seen you around here before. You gnu to this neighborhood?"

"Yeah," Agnu replied, "I'm a gnucomer."

"Where ya from?"

Agnu hesitated. "I just got out of Gnu Haven." He gave a mirthless laugh. "Haven? Hell, it was more like a prison. High fences all around. Closed gates. I gnu there had to be a better place than that somewhere so I busted out."

"How'd ya do that?" a bar patron sitting next to him asked.

"One day when the gnusboy opened a gate to deliver the gnuspaper I made a run for it."

"Hey, you're an escapee," the bartender yelled. "I run a clean joint here and I don't want no trouble with the cops."

"I'm innocent of any crime," Agnu protested. "I was living peacefully on the African veldt when a big Gnubian roped me. He sold me to a guy who took me to Gnu Haven."

"You're a long way from Gnu Haven. Why did you come here?" the bartender asked.

Agnu sighed. "It's a long story. I ended up here by accident. At first I thought I might go north to Gnufoundland, but I decided it's too cold there. Cold weather is hard on my gnuralgia and gnuritis. Also, I could catch gnumonia there. At Gnu Haven I went to the gnurologist. He said it's all in my imagination, that I'm just gnurotic. A lot he knows. I get pains in gnumerous places every day."

"So you headed south?"

217

AGNU'S RUN

"I hopped aboard a Gnu York Central freight train and ended up in the big city. As I was trotting down Fifth Avengnu, minding my own business, a bunch of guys in blue uniforms began chasing me. I guess they thought I was trying to hook up with a herd of gnubile gnudes and make a lot of gnu babies to dump on their welfare system. Talk about profiling!"

He gave a hollow laugh. "They could have saved themselves the trouble. I'm gnutral, if you know what I mean."

"Gnutral?"

Agnu exploded. "Do I have to spell it out? At Gnu Haven they gnutered me."

"Hey," the bartender quickly apologized, "I didn't mean to get personal. So what happened after the Gnu York cops chased you?"

"I ran to the docks and jumped aboard a ship that was just pulling out. I stowed away. While the ship was at sea I overheard a crewman say they were headed for Gnuport Gnus, Virginia, so I guess that's where I am."

"Yeah, you're in Gnuport Gnus," the bar patron replied. "Hey, where'd ya get that big bump on your noggin?"

Agnu touched his scalp gingerly. "I sat under a tree to rest and an apple bonked me." He managed a wry smile. "I guess that Gnuton fellow gnu what he was tanking about. I ate the apple. Apples are very gnutritious."

"Well, it did a job on your head. So where do ya go from here?"

For a long moment Agnu remained silent before answering. "I'm beginning to think a gnu life outside Gnu Haven is not for me. At least I didn't go hungry there. I'm going back."

"You hungry?" the bartended asked. "I got some good Gnu England clam chowder."

"I got no money."

"Hey, after what you been through it's on the house." He

AGNU'S RUN

paused. "Ya gonna take a plane back?"

"No," Agnu shook his head, "I got no faith in those gnufangled flying machines. Besides, I go no money and it's almost impossible to get past Security and hitch a ride. They think everybody is a terrorist trying to sneak a gnuclear device aboard."

He looked imploringly at the bartender. "I don't want to be a gnuisance, but is it okay if I stay here the rest of the night? Then I'll see what the gnu day brings."

A SAILOR'S LAMENT
(ballad in Malayan form pantoum)

The day that I put out to sea
my one true love I left behind
she swore to God her love for me
and it did give me peace of mind.

My one true love I left behind
she filled my dreams with acts of love
and it did give me peace of mind
she'd made a pact with God above.

She filled my dreams with acts of love
through stormy weeks and months at sea
she'd made a pact with God above
I knew that she'd be true to me.

Through stormy weeks and months at sea
on her my lonely heart would dwell
I knew that she'd be true to me
her faithful heart I knew so well.

On her my lonely mind would dwell
I longed to have her in my bed
her faithful heart I knew so well
but then another she did wed.

I longed to have her in my bed
she swore to God her love for me
but then another she did wed
the day that I put out to sea.

A Malayan form pantoum consists of any number of four-line stanzas. The 2nd and 4th lines of each are repeated as the 1st and 3rd lines of the next stanza. The 3rd line of the first stanza is repeated as the 2nd line of the last stanza. The first line of the first stanza is repeated as the last line of the last stanza.